In fierce determination, Doctor Preston Sumner lived up to that secret, unspoken reputation which every dentist is afraid he may have. Pangs of torment ripped through his patients' gums. Agony leaped from their incisors. Their wisdom teeth were wrenched out at awkward angles that left nerves singing like a chorus of the damned.

Preston Sumner did not betray his profession casually.

It was the promise of immortality that had seduced him.

And the promise seemed to be working. . . .

THE DENTIST

by J. N. Williamson

A DELL/EMERALD BOOK

This is a work of fiction. All the characters and events portrayed in this book are fictional, and any resemblance to real people or incidents is purely coincidental.

Published by
Dell Publishing Co., Inc.
1 Dag Hammarskjold Plaza
New York, New York 10017

Copyright © 1983 by J. N. Williamson

All rights reserved. No part of this book may be reproduced or transmitted in any form or by any means, electronic or mechanical, including photocopying, recording or by any information storage and retrieval system, without the written permission of the Publisher, except where permitted by law.

Dell ® TM 681510, Dell Publishing Co., Inc.

ISBN: 0-440-01792-0

Printed in the United States of America

First printing—October, 1983

For my wife and agent Mary, whose life refutes Lincoln—she is blessedly uncommon and she manages to be everything at all times to many people—and for my father Lynn Williamson, quite literally my earliest supporter.

". . . My eyes are heavy, my arms are feeble, my legs will not move, my heart is slow. Death draws nigh to me, soon shall they lead me to the city of eternity.
 Does not the eye fear, which looks upon thee?"
—"Tale of Sinuhe," Egyptian Tales,
Translated by William Flinders Petrie

PROLOGUE

"The first idea that the child must acquire, in order to be actively disciplined, is that of the difference between good and evil . . ."
—Maria Montessori

"You are to have as strict a guard upon yourself amongst your children, as if you were amongst your enemies."
—Lord Halifax (1633–1695)

Nine years ago in a small Indiana town.

Ruben Memorial Hospital was scarcely larger than a clinic but shiny-new, and they liked to do things their way. After

Ginny delivered and they were sure the first-time mother was out of danger, they wheeled her back to her own room. Familiarity and comfort, they reasoned, got a patient back on her feet more quickly than the austere whiteness of the recovery room. Consequently, her street clothes were hung in full view, encouragingly; a photo montage from home was on the wall; and there was a bed to be used, one night, by her husband.

In her room, then, beneath a bouquet of real flowers sent by Alan and a bouquet of crisp artificial ones that had seen two-dozen other new mothers regain consciousness, Ginny groped her way up through the internal shroud of fog and blinked with mild apprehension when she saw her surroundings.

Had she really had the baby? Was it all right?

Alan sat in a nearby chair, a snoozing lighthouse in the murk fading from her thoughts. He was exhausted, his eyes shut, but—like always—he was *there*. There, when Ginny needed him.

For most of her twenty years Ginny had been a person who felt no need for numbers of people—acquaintances—preferring, instead, a few fully-intimate relationships. Individual affection, not crowds with smirking brittle smiles which pretended to like her, gave Ginny a sense of belonging.

And after one grand year of being closer to the young newspaperman, Alan Simmons, than she had ever believed it possible to be, Ginny longed now for the ultimate close connection: that which a mother might enjoy with her baby. It was the reason she planned to breast-feed this, her first offspring—to establish an intimate bond that would endure forever.

Whatever might happen to Alan or her in a world which

THE DENTIST

sometimes seemed full of devilish pits lined with piercing stakes, a world that had always offered a Cheshire-cat grin and (so Ginny believed) held poisoned daggers behind its collective back, a son meant there would always be that one human being you could unstintingly trust. A younger, obedient, more needful and controllable human being who cared about things like love and family, shared experiences, honesty and giving.

Whenever her pregnancy had been at its most confining, awkward, or painful, Ginny had consistently comforted herself with a vivid image of the unseen child peacefully, trustingly suckling at her swollen, newly-nourishing breasts. It had sent her sailing through all the shoals of the difficult nine months and now, now that the child could be seen, Ginny was impatient to hold it in her arms.

When he heard his name whispered, Alan was instantly on his feet, leaning over Ginny with his modishly-long light-brown hair dangling in his concerned eyes. "Are you okay? How d'you feel, darlin'?"

She closed her eyes briefly. "I'm fine." She took his kiss gladly, aware that she probably had breath like a sewer, and gently pushed him up. "The baby," she said anxiously. "Is it—all right?"

The hesitation was so transient, so flickeringly slight, Ginny wasn't really sure she'd seen more than a glint in Alan's eyes. "Sweetheart, we did it!" he enthused. "We had ourselves a boy! Luke Simmons, just the way we planned him!"

She patted his face happily. "Where is he? When are they bringing him to me?" she asked.

Alan didn't answer. He was still smiling at her but his

eyes had stopped laughing and they'd stopped glinting. It looked like he was afraid to lift his gaze from her, to break the moment; because when that happened, they'd have to go on to all the other moments. "They didn't know my girl would be up and around so soon," he answered, tearing his eyes away from her face. "I'm sure they'll be here with Luke in a moment."

Alan looked so *pale*, all at once. She still had hold of his hand and she squeezed the fingers unmercifully, the nails pricking. "Where is my little boy?" she demanded. "Alan, is there something *wrong* with him?"

His eyes grazed hers before slipping past. "Not exactly," he told her. He cleared his throat and added, as if that explained everything, "There's not exactly *anything* wrong with him." He didn't quite know what to say. He wanted them to bring Luke to her, let her see for herself. Maybe, Alan thought, I'm exaggerating the importance of it in my own mind. I'm probably blowing everything out of proportion.

When the doctor, Adam Bridell, softly entered the room with something bundled in blue softness against his suit, Ginny cried out with sudden sharp knowing. It should not be the doctor bringing Luke to her, she realized. That was the nurse's job. The doctor wouldn't be here unless—*unless something was wrong with the baby!*

The man stopped at her bed, stiff and impeccable in his expensive suit, his reddish face expressionless. He placed the baby beside her and parted the blanket so she could see him.

"What's w-wrong with him?" Ginny asked, unable to touch the tiny infant. Her green eyes pleaded with Dr. Bridell. "Doctor, *tell* me! *What's wrong with m-my baby?*"

"Madam," he replied, make-believe stiffness and offense

raising his immaculate shoulders, "how dare you imply that one of the children *I* delivered could have anything 'wrong' with it?" Then he laughed reassuringly, a snorting noise, and broadly gestured with his hands above the quiet infant. "Take a close look if you don't believe me."

Ginny bobbed her head, glanced with a mixture of curiosity and wounded insult at her husband Alan, and took a close look. In the age-old way of mothers, in the most ancient physical evaluation in the world, she instinctively studied the child's minutiae, risking a mother's most terrifying noun: *freak*. She didn't look first at tiny Luke's face but prodded his plump flesh like a finger inserted in the Pilsbury Doughboy, counted his fingers and toes, gingerly raised his microscopic genitalia—

And finally, conscious of how her breasts were just beginning to fill, she lifted her frightened but critical gaze to the boy-child's face:

He had Alan's widely-separated and neatly linear brows: they seemed drawn-on, in light mascara. Blinking, Little Luke reflexively opened his cloudy eyes and Ginny squealed, glancing up at Doctor Bridell.

"It's almost the rule," he said promptly, "not the exception, for a newborn to be crosseyed."

Yet, Ginny saw, he remained close to her bedside. She gently massaged the fuzzy, golden fringe of hair. His forehead was offputting, wrinkled as it was like some old man remembering the Depression. Like a customer kicking used-car tires, she peeped behind Luke's ears and ended by chucking him under the chin.

New to this world, Luke Simmons parted his hungry lips at once in an utterly grotesque and gassy grin. To Ginny's horror, the smirk revealed—pointy and shining like stalactites and stalagmites in the cavern of his moist mouth—three adult-like, perfect, stunningly inappropriate teeth. Two, fangish and vulpine, above; one, gross and incredibly large, below. With his clouded crossed eyes slightly open but staring and blind, the trio of incredible teeth gave to Luke that moment the appearance of some balding alien from the dark side of the moon.

"He has *teeth*!" Ginny cried, wrenching her hands from the newborn.

"It's not *that* unusual," Doctor Bridell murmured, shrugging, tasting his dry lips with the tip of his tongue.

It's not your baby, Ginny thought with ferocity. Her husband Alan, a wordsmith and dealer in images, pictured a skinny standup comic with graying hair and a worshipful crowd calling, *How unusual is it, Johnny?* Alan swallowed. "How often does this h-happen?" he inquired.

"Hard to say." The physician expelled air as he considered. "At least as unusual as one in five-hundred births, possibly as rare as one in a thousand." He warned them with his raised index finger. "But there are thousands of babies born every day. That means quite a few of them have a tooth or two." He laughed with the sound of a choking thoroughbred. "Look at it this way. He'll be able to eat solids faster than most children."

"Doctor." It was Ginny. She tugged his sleeve for attention. "Can I—can I still breast-feed my baby?"

"Of course," he answered promptly. Then, staring down at the new mother, he added, "Well, you'll have to be very careful, of course," he amended his reply. "I suppose it might be quite painful at times. You might experiment with

THE DENTIST

it, see how it goes, before committing yourself to full-time breast-feeding."

"Get out," she said softly. When no one moved, Ginny's glance scalded their faces—both Doctor Bridell and her husband Alan, each male, each uncomprehending. "Please, both of you, get out awhile. Leave me with my baby."

Alan's face asked the other man a question. He nodded, catching Alan's elbow and leading him toward the door. "It's all right," he told the new father. "They just need time to get acquainted."

Ginny stared at the door. When she was sure they were gone, she slipped the nightgown to one side, freeing one puffy, blue-veined breast. It was moist at its apex. She cupped the baby under one arm, lifted him closer and closer toward her readied nipple.

Suddenly Ginny stopped. She paused, then lay the baby on the sheets. Luke was beginning to make fussing sounds in the base of his throat. It sounded to her almost like a small dog growling. She blinked two or three times, staring at the baby, and then poked out at him with her index finger.

He took it happily into his mouth, with sucking movements of the lips.

Almost immediately Ginny screamed involuntarily. Tears leaped to her eyes. She tried to pull the finger out of her baby's mouth but he held on for dear life, his jaws clamping down and grinding, his hot little tongue brushing the fingertip like a moving piece of liver.

Wounded, Ginny felt nauseous. She felt partly *digested*. With her free hand, she squeezed the newborn's cheeks together, and pulled.

With a popping sound the finger came free and Ginny gaped at it with horror.

It dripped blood from the nail past the first joint. It looked . . . chewed . . . with the flesh around the bitten area laid back and seeping, almost as though some kind of animal had done this awful thing.

Quickly, she covered her bare breast with the gauzy cloth of the gown. Baby Luke began crying. The noises were relentlessly demanding. Ginny looked at him, saw her blood on the baby's lips, shuddered.

"It only means you're bound to be remarkable in lots of ways, my little son," she told him when she could, her voice catching. "You're going to be very very very bright, and very good, and very special to mommy, aren't you, darling?" She stuck her index finger in her mouth and sucked on it, the taste at once metallic and sickeningly something of hotblooded humankind. Around it, she beseeched Luke Simmons a final time: *"Aren't you?"*

ONE

They were part of the new cave-dwelling generation, young marrieds clustered in paperwalled apartments like grapes, adrift in an economic epilogue to the genuine history of their fathers and grandfathers. They could not speak of their big brothers, who had only avoidance of Viet Nam to mention instead of the Berlins and Tokyos and 32nd Parallels and Pork Chop Hills of their elders; and while their fathers lived, they were merely disapprovingly booming echoes whose compassionate blood had all run away in defiance of queer creations like Hitler, Mussolini, Tojo and something called "geeks."

Valiantly striving to raise their children in what was suitably called a "complex," soothed by drugs and instantly rattled by fear for the illegality of it, these young marrieds were forever obliged to measure-up to shadows and never quite sure they were casting their own. On those that might have been, the next generation that was their own offspring, they lavished the benediction of orthodontics, ten-speed bicycles, complicated stereos on which to hear simpleminded sound, little league hockey and soccer, and a sort-of roughhouse camaraderie lacking in their childhood.

They lived, these people who knew they'd never see a dime of their social security investment and tacitly accepted the likelihood of raining nuclear radiation, in a place called Stevenson, Indiana. Identical in most prominent ways to ten thousand others, it was one of the newer suburban creations lacking the shared commonplace of a local factory and the detached mutuality of big-city crime and crowding. When anyone called the police in tiny Stevenson, it was for narcotics-gone-wild, tidy domestic murder, one of the countless apartment break-ins leaving young mothers gray before they were thirty, or because their jerrybuilt structures were afire again. Upwardly mobile with a doggedness easily surpassing their fathers' post-war ambitions, but less admirable, they tended to platoon-like assemblages in their curb-parked cars each morning and an all-out surge toward big-city Indianapolis. Most of the drivers were young enough that they emulated, ineptly, their idols of the Speedway 500 Mile Race; in May, an inexperienced driver took his life in his hands to mingle with them on I-70 or 465.

And on Saturday nights, when their dads and grandpas nostalgically claimed to have heard *Don't Sit Under the Apple Tree, You Belong to Me, Wish You Were Here,* or even *Lily*

The Dentist

Marlene in USO clubs or teary-and-beery foreign bars in a thousand exotically bombed-out cities, the modern cave-dwellers drove one block to the apartment complex clubhouse. There, like as not, some cold-steel stereo symbol of Nowness cut the smoky air like a laser and drummed-out the taunting reverberations of what their fathers and grandfathers had left them.

It was summer now in Stevenson and none of the young marrieds or their children, bounding like bunnies from one corner of the clubhouse to the other, wore more clothing than the law demanded. It was still early and no one was drunk yet, though half the men in the place were willing. A few had begun the Saturday night festivities at home, puffing on joints. Now their shrill, pointlessly-laughing voices sounded periodically above the music like cornet solos. The clubhouse itself consisted of a foyer and two main rooms, one with a fireplace, the other with a bar tended by one of the neighbors—a Mr. Michaels—who needed part-time income. During the winter, dwellers of the Knightsbury complex settled near the former; but this was summer, the fireplace was soberingly unkindled, and the front room mostly contained youngsters and prudent young wives who'd have to get unsteady husbands home, later.

In point of fact, Alan Simmons was the only adult male in the room, seated beside his darkhaired wife Ginny. Restless, his gaze swept the other people and barely identified them: Cort Devalyn's four kids, hollering over a Crazy Eights game on a nearby table; enticing Liz Douglas, the new redhead at Knightsbury, her breasts due to pop-out of their halter any minute; his and Ginny's son, Luke, currently watching Mr. Michaels' every motion as if he yearned to become a bartender.

Alan's attitude wasn't so much downcast as charged with the electricity of frustration.

Ginny intuited as much but wanted him to get it out. "What's the matter, hon?"

He turned to her, his face still boyish at thirty—more so since he'd finally summoned the independence to have his light-brown hair cut short. Whenever she asked him that question, relenting, his small, gray eyes became earnest with internal hurt. He had a way of licking the right corner of his mouth before replying, as if giving himself a second more to gain control of his vagrant moods. "This morning I felt there was a good chance that suicide story I wrote for *Subjects* would get picked up by the *News*." "*Subjects*" was *Hoosier Subjects*, the suburban weekly for which he was a grossly underpaid reporter; "News" was the Indianapolis *News*, one of the big city's two dailies. "A few good pieces printed there and they might take me on. But Willie Dean at the *News* killed it. Liked my use of stats, he told Ernie at *Subjects*, but the story was crowded-out by some looting in the Indy inner city."

For a moment Ginny didn't answer. She lay back in her chair, her rather long legs bare below shorts and raised to a hassock. Her generous, tanned thighs rolled like hillocks and she met Alan's gaze with old, cherished sympathy and touched his hand. "You'll get your break someday, sweetheart," she told him in a soft voice that kept it from others in the clubhouse. "You told me Willie is getting up there and that they like to hire competent people from smaller papers. Like a baseball farm team. This is only another delay, that's all."

Alan nodded vaguely and glanced down at his familiar jeans—there was no logo or design on the hip pocket; most of the Simmons clothes came from Target or K-Mart—and touched his cold drink to his temple. His tongue dampened the right corner of his mouth. "God, it's hot tonight!" he observed. Again he turned to face her, a journalistic Peter Pan, and kissed Ginny's slightly sloping nose. "Thanks for keeping the faith."

"Whoa, dammit; hold it! Enough of that filthy sex-jazz!"

It was Ellie Devalyn before their embarrassed grins, the chubby blonde they'd known since they were all in Stevenson High together, with Ellie's husband Cort. Without being fat, everything about goodhumored Ellie was round: her face, her meaty breasts, her belly, buttocks, thighs and kneecaps. Her smile was a constant half-circle set prettily beneath a round button nose and her eyes were limpid pools of quickwitted sensitivity.

She slipped with surprising grace into a chair beside Ginny. She, too, wore shorts, but the effect fell far short of Ginny's, a fact Ellie had ceased to mind ten years ago. She noticed the way they were holding hands and lifted both brows. "I always said this wouldn't work," she said. "Aries and Scorpio are dissociate signs; they don't have a thing in common unless it's their joint Mars rulership."

"Oh, Lord," Alan sighed in mock resentment. "Here she goes again. 'Madame Futura, the See-All Know-It-All. Your Stars and Coat Checked While you Wait.' "

Ellie stuck her tongue out at him. "When you're the only woman in the bunch who doesn't work, loudmouthed Arian, you got to have *something* to occupy your time." She folded her arms across her ample chest. "And *I* had the commonsense to learn everything there was to know in the whole world."

Alan gave her a grin but it turned rueish halfway through. "You wouldn't be the only nonworking wife if I could just get on with the *News*," he observed. "The way things are, I have to smooch Ginny up now and then. Her part-time job at Fast-First Foto buys most of the hamburger." He paused to cast a look around the clubhouse. "Where's your genius of a husband, El? I saw Brian and your other three little hellions scampering by a few minutes ago. Cort can't be far behind."

"He'll be along in a moment, I'm sure." Ellie bit her lip and appeared to be deciding how much to say about something. "I've been concerned about ole Cort lately, kids. He's drinking more than usual." She saw that Alan was about to speak and held her palm up. "Whoa, pal, let me finish. If he was just starting to hit the bottle a little, I'd know what to do. Besides, he's too smart a guy to let himself become a drunk. If it was *just* drinking, I wouldn't be too concerned."

"Well, what is it?" Ginny asked, sitting up to face her old friend. She was not only much prettier than Ellie, she was taller. Confronting the blonde from the same seated position, Ginny was reminded of how short-waisted Ellie was. "Maybe we can help. We go back a long way with Cort."

"Right," Alan put in, placing his drink on a coffee table. "Is there something wrong at that school where he teaches?"

"Good old Von Braun High, where the little genius kiddies unlike us matriculate instead of masturbate?" She guffawed at her own joke. "They say it's the only school in Indiana with both brains and 'braun.' No, he's just teaching a couple of classes during summer vacation." Her eyes grew larger. "It's hard to put your finger on it, actually; but Cort

22

has something on his mind." She hesitated, "Kids, Cort is changing."

"Maybe it's his friendship with that dentist, Press Summer," Ginny said, making a face. "I can't for the life of me imagine what he sees in the man."

Alan chuckled. "She's never been able to stand dentists, El," he explained. "Has a theory that every last one of 'em is a secret sadist, that they got into dentistry just to cause people pain." He rested his palm on Ginny's thigh. "Honey, we don't want to talk behind Press' back that way. Not when we've all started going to him. It never pays to make policemen, doctors, grass-dealers and dentists mad."

"Everything okay?"

They turned their heads to discover Luke, their one child, near at hand. Always a cooperative child, he nonetheless had the disconcerting habit of standing only inches from his mother and father, virtually materializing there. It made them think of their possible needs for mouthwash and deodorant. Alan had decided Luke needed glasses. He'd been right, and Luke always wore them these days; but the nine-year-old still approached them like a lithe little leopard.

"We're fine, darling," Ginny answered him, puzzled. "Why do you ask?"

"I drinking a coke and watchin Mr. Michaels mix drinks. I thought I saw funny looks on your faces." He shrugged. On this humid Saturday evening, Luke had slipped into a rather autumnish pullover and wore jeans instead of the fringed shorts worn by Ellie's boys. He gave his parents a discomfited grin, his teeth gleaming in the light from the overhead chandelier. "Didn't mean t'interrupt."

When he had moved away, seemingly with no sound, Ellie touched Ginny's arm and frowned. "Your boy is right, as usual. Gin, didn't you say you couldn't imagine what Cort *sees* in Press?"

Ginny paused, her lips parting. "Why, I guess I did. But—"

"Maybe I'm touchy, but I believe that's the kind of question someone raises about a man and a woman." Ellie extracted her hand from Ginny's arm and looked away, angrily. "I'll grant you it's sudden, the way my Cort and *Doctor* Preston Sumner have become inseparable pals. But if you mean to *imply*—"

"No, no," Ginny answered, appalled. "I didn't mean—"

"Because my Cort is all-man, if nothing else."

Ginny nodded, hard. When Ellie was peeved, the way she was now, her fairskinned blondeness appeared to turn silver and gray, adding years to her own twenty-nine. It occurred to Alan that if she ever truly lost her temper, she'd bleach out into a simple undefined swath of faded nothingness.

"He's odd, but he's not queer," she added. "D'you know what I mean?"

Before either Simmons could answer, she was up and moving through the clubhouse, stopping to talk with an apartment complex couple, Mary and Dennis Grazell. Their daughter, Alaina, scarcely two, took one look at Ellie and began to cry. She scooped the child up and began talking baby-talk to her.

"Now, what the hell was all *that* about?" Alan murmured, surprised. "The last thing I'd believe about Cort was that he was gay."

"Me, too," Ginny replied. Then, looking for Luke and seeing that he was talking with Brian Devalyn, fourteen, on a level of equality, her glance fell on someone tall who was approaching. She elbowed Alan. "Speak of the devil."

Cort Devalyn, Alan's classmate through four years of high school in Stevenson, resembled nothing so much as a scholarly crane. Walking toward them with his usual amused smirk on his lips, clad in a long-sleeved white shirt and the walking shorts that he wore in almost every kind of weather, Cort was over six-four in height and didn't outweigh middlesized Alan Simmons by five pounds.

But other than the height, what one tended to notice about the teacher of anthropology were his brightly-gleaming brown eyes that were larger behind thick-lensed, hornrimmed glasses, and his excessive slenderness. The eyes tended to stare; once, years ago in school, Ginny had thought they were calculating until she discovered his deliciously offbeat sense of humor. The legs, naked in his shorts, ran fleshlessly up-and-down without a bulge, like mobile exclamation marks.

"Well-l-l, hi," he drawled in his oddly amiable but self-conscious tenor. He stooped to kiss Ginny on the cheek, all elbows. "Glad you two are here."

Alan remembered Ellie's concern and asked, testingly, "Where's your drink? It's not like you to be here this long without a cold one."

Cort's brown eyes flickered with annoyance. "I don't drink much anymore," he said a trifle curtly. "It affects my thinking and I have a serious project I'm working on during the summer hiatus."

Ginny's gaze met Alan's with surprise. "How long is 'anymore'?" she asked as merrily as possible.

Cort Devalyn was looking around, head revolving on the thin stalk of his long neck. "Last two days or so," he replied, abstractedly. "Time shouldn't be measured by the clock, right? I mean, the proper measuring stick is how deeply one gets involved in worthwhile projects to the exclusion of everything else. —Have you two seen Press?"

"Why, no," Alan said slowly, uncrossing his legs and recrossing them. "Something special up? Does your new project involve him in some way?"

Cort's head ducked back to normal length. He smiled affably and suddenly giggled, clearly embarrassed. "Gee, I'm ashamed to admit it after making such a pretentious remark. It's just that Press and I plan to go hunting tomorrow morning."

"You never used to hunt," Ginny remarked. "You said it was senseless waste to go around killing harmless little animals. I remember you said that man was the only animal who both hunted and killed for amusement."

The anthropology teacher sighed. He still hadn't taken a seat, and their necks were beginning to hurt from smiling up at him. He rested a wide hand on Alan's shoulder. "That was before I learned how a great, natural hunter handles himself."

"Press?" Alan asked, surprised. An image of the short, stocky dentist with his foul-smelling cigars twinkled like a star in his mind.

"Press," Cort nodded, definitively. "You have to look closely at old Press to appreciate him. Still waters run deep. He's a truly marvelous hunter, Alan. He has a remarkable grasp of psychology—animals and humans both. I mean, it's a privilege to see him at work." Cort lifted his free hand and dramatically painted the picture. "There you are in the woods where every tree looks like every other tree, all the grass and weeds are alike. I swear, Alan, Ginny, that little man thinks pre*ci*sely the way an animal thinks." The tall man's eyes glowed with admiration. "He . . . *gets into their skins*, finds their vulnerable points. Before they ever show themselves, he knows where to aim his rifle—with infinite patience. I've seen him hit rabbit and quail the *instant* their muscles put them into motion."

"My God," Ginny whispered, picturing the bird plunge to the ground, the bleeding rabbit twitching helplessly on its side.

"Yes, it's beautiful to see," Cort said with enthusiasm. Then he caught their expressions and shrugged. "Maybe you have to be there to appreciate it. Would you go with us some morning, Alan?"

"No," the newspaper man answered, looking away, "thank you. I prefer bunny rabbits and beautiful deer with their clothes still on. The only time I like naked animals is when they're on my plate disguised as food."

Cort didn't hear. He was staring at the door. Then he seemed to float absent-mindedly away. Alan whispered, "Ellie's right. Cort is changing."

"He certainly is," she agreed. "But in just what way, I can't for the life of me say." Suddenly she tugged at his sleeve. "Let's go apologize to Ellie. I don't like leaving her with hurt feelings."

"I didn't make that crack about Cort and Press," Alan

grumbled, pulling himself to his feet. He was generally serious-minded, a person who remembered to wear a winning smile at all occasions and who disliked being around large groups of people. It was one of the things he'd had in common with Ginny, and one of the reasons he'd encouraged Cort and Ellie, when they returned to Stevenson for a nostalgic visit, to stay. Their ties went back far enough, and covered enough common experiences, that Alan could relax around them. "It was you who opened mouth, inserted foot."

"I need your husbandly support, shortie," Ginny snapped, pulling him by the arm. She enjoyed the fact that he was only an inch or so taller and, since Luke was born nine years ago, that he was only sixteen pounds heavier than she. She added, in an English accent borrowed from the *Duchess of Duke Street*, "Come along, gov'ner, there's a good ole chap!"

The apology was accepted quickly and returned in kind. Ellie Devalyn hugged Ginny, kissed her old friend on the cheek. "It's astrology again, kids," she said by way of explanation. "I'm being Twelfth Housed by the start of the damned Leo period. I should have known you weren't so petty."

"But you were right about one thing," Alan told her, fetching drinks for both women. "Cort seems to be changing, or at least changeable."

"*Something* is going on," Ellie said, nodding. "And in our very own group." She lowered her voice to speak closely to Ginny's ear. "Personally, I think it's strange the way Press' wife Angela left him last week. She'd finally been accepted by most of us and then she simply disappeared. Nobody much cares for Press, but Angela's really a sweet little thing."

Ginny glanced at Alan, then plunged. "To tell the truth, Ellie, she called me. I know where she took their daughter, little Lucy, but she made me *swear* not to tell anybody where they were. And that's peculiar too."

Ellie's eyes glittered knowingly. "That's right, you and Angela particularly hit it off, didn't you? You were the first to see Angela on her own merits as a person, despite her dull husband."

Ginny finished her drink in a gulp. "I'm no libber, hon, but I'm also no extension of my own husband. I wouldn't want people to think I was a nothing simply because *he* was!"

"Hey!" Alan exclaimed, smacking her rump. "Be a little more careful about the way you draw your analogies, will ya?"

"Poor little booper," Ginny hissed, kissing him full on the lips with a giggle. "Did mommy hurt ums feelings?"

"Just don't compare me to Press," Alan said hotly. "He's a damned good dentist—we both have check-ups this Wednesday, by the way—but he sure flunked out of charm school! And besides, I suspect Cort may be right. I think the little creep is full of secrets."

Luke appeared beside them with a tray bearing refills. "I mixed these myself," he said proudly, raising the tray. "I watched Mr. Michaels do it, for a long time, and then he let me try. Here."

Alan frowned faintly. How did the poor kid always manage to show up at the worst moment? "I just finished a drink, son. You don't want your old man to fall flat on his face, do you?"

Ginny made a face at him. "Spoilsport," she said, taking the glass meant for her. "Ellie?"

Ellie paused, then took the proffered cocktail. With a sigh, Alan accepted his own. Over Luke's tousled head he saw that Press had arrived, that he and Cort were approaching, joining Cort's wife Ellie.

They were a Mutt-and-Jeff combination, the tall and short of it, Alan mused. Dr. Preston Sumner was only slightly taller than an unemployable midget, approximately the height of Cort's fourteen-year-old Brian, but with such a steady, inflexible bearing that he appeared larger. The same age as the others, his hair was thinning on top, he had eyes the color of bonfire smoke lurking beneath heavy spectacles, and a mouth with lips that didn't move even when he spoke. Stocky of build with chunky, hairy forearms strengthened from years of pulling and treating teeth, he affected fist-sized stogies. A cloud of blue-gray smoke trailed in his path, reminding Alan of a lonely engineer's cab puffing powerfully down a railroad track. There was, the writer mused, something of the *perpetual* about Press Sumner, something that was meant to remain stubbornly the same for a lifetime and then settled into the ground like the stump of a burnt-out tree.

He only had time to accept Sumner's sturdy handshake before Luke was again injecting his small self into the conversation. "Tell Uncle Cort and Aunt Ellie and Uncle Press about what happened at school!" he entreated them with an engaging, wide grin.

"We're really very proud of our Luke," Ginny told the others, stooping to kiss his forehead. "He's attended summer school only because he has such a hunger for knowledge, for facts. And he had a chance to have his IQ professionally tested." She rumpled his hair and beamed on him. "You know, ever since Luke was born with three little teeth we've known he was an unusual child. I always believed he'd make us proud of him one day."

Alan, looking down at his son, heard a sharp, sibilant sound. He looked up but couldn't tell which of their three friends had sounded startled. Lanky Cort Devalyn looked intrigued. "Do tell us the results of Luke's testing."

"Well, it was one of those genuine collegiate IQ evaluations generally administered at Badler U." He smiled. "To make a long story short, ole Lukey tested-out as a bonafide genius!"

"Isn't—that—something?" Cort said. He touched Luke's cheek with approving, long fingers.

"You must be very proud of him," Ellie said, hugging Luke against her ampleness.

Press Sumner spoke for the first time. He had the deep, flat-toned voice that made instant listeners of those who heard it. Unfortunately, they tended eventually to conclude that he really had nothing to say and that what the little man *did* say was both dogmatic and clumsily expressed. It was, Alan thought, as if Press saw so many tangents and ramifications in even the simplest thought, when he discussed it his mouth could not decide what road to follow. To the best of the reporter's knowledge, Cort was the only friend Press had in the world. "I think you should bring Luke with you to my office on Wednesday," he said, and it was a statement, not a request. The deep-set eyes behind his thick lenses fixed heavily on Ginny's face. "You can't begin good oral hygiene at too early an age, you know."

Luke looked up at Alan, his own glasses clouding. "Can I go, Dad? I've been readin a little about dentistry. They tried to keep teeth in good shape all the way back to the Etruscans and before." His smile was boyish, ingenuous in its openness, despite his surprising request. "Except, back then, false teeth were *real* teeth."

Alan frowned. "How can that be, son?"

"They ripped 'em right out of the mouths of slaves!" Luke retorted, laughing.

Cort Devalyn peered curiously down at the boy, his long, thin face admiring. When his redhaired son Brian and his other three children drew near, he looked at the fourteen-year-old with gloomy disapproval. "I'd give almost anything if you demonstrated a mere *iota* of the interest in knowledge displayed by this little boy," he said acidly.

"Cort!" Ellie exclaimed, flushing, seeing the wounded expression on young Brian's face. "Don't you *ever* compare our children to another one! It's entirely unfair. It's—it's specious, too."

" 'Specious?' " repeated the tall teacher. He smiled sardonically at his plump wife. "Well, what d'you know? I'm fairly wading in an ocean of wisdom after all." He looked down again, ignoring Ellie to slap little Luke on the shoulder. "You're quite right about the Etruscans, you know. But we've outgrown such prehistoric claptrap." His gaze met the dentist's and held. "Remember, our Press is a painless dentist. It never bothers him a bit."

Everyone laughed at the old joke but Alan, who shuddered, and then wondered why. He had wandered a few steps away to place his drink on the bar and glanced back at the group, now, sensing . . . *currents* . . . between his old friend Cort and the stocky, silent dentist. What was it Ellie said of her husband? "Cort has *something* on his mind. Cort is changing." And she'd added, later, *"Something is going on."*

But what? Alan frowned. What could it be? And *why*, when it was such a sweltering summer night, did he suddenly feel the chilling fingers of an unseen hand running the length of his spine? Was there really anything to be worried about—and was it really any business of his, anyway?

TWO

Eleven P.M.

Sitting on the edge of the bed, Angela Sumner brushed her little girl's hair with smooth, sweeping motions that stretched to tiny Lucy's waistline. This was one of their old, private rituals, this sharing of the obvious thing they had in common: beautiful, deep auburn hair that was very nearly red and, when morning sunshine struck it just so, was. Angela's was trimmed to shoulder length, however, and Lucy, scarcely five, enjoyed demanding—amid giggles—whether mommy's hair would "be long when she was a big girl, too."

It had seemed wise to Angela, after she left Preston Sumner, to maintain as many of the old family customs as she could. Although she was an accepting, phlegmatic sort of woman herself, Angela was smart enough to realize how traumatic sweeping changes could be for a child.

For herself, however, there had never seemed to be enough in life that was either ecstatically fulfilling or deeply painful. Nothing of the potential suicide had ever existed for a minute inside her red head, because of the way she viewed life: A droning sequence of events over which she had little control, and even less desire to gain the upper hand. Her outlook, almost always, was live-and-let-live; she refused to get excited even when her own interests were thwarted.

Except once.

That was why, to the absolute surprise of those who merely thought they knew her well, Angela had married Press, six years ago. To them, it appeared an abject waste. After all, the still-youthful redhead earned a decent income from her work as an interior decorator and knew lots of men who were cultured, successful, and handsome. When her acquaintances saw balding, miniature, serious-minded and plodding Preston Sumner, they thought Angela had lost her mind.

But the reasons for her choice were quite clear to Angela. She had been married before, in another city, to a man named Roger Crosby who was wonderously handsome, successful, publicly cultured—and a demanding brute who haunted her dreams. Roger used drugs, in the privacy of their home, for the eleven months of their marriage. Amphetamines. And when they had him high enough, Roger always took one of two roads: he either insisted on all

THE DENTIST

varieties of fantasy-laden, kinky and sometimes painful sex, or insisted on beating Angela to a pulp.

Yet the narrower reason her first marriage didn't last was what Roger—successful, cultured, handsome Roger—did to her shortly before the one and final breakup. He asked a horrid little creature named Artie "the Kid" Kinkaid to share their bed. Angela went along with it, once, losing forever some vital strand of pride and acquiring an indigestible memory of immense self-loathing. After that, she refused, and the two choices of meanness on handsome, cultured Roger's part changed. He either thrashed her, often without the assistance of uppers, or kicked her into the living room and spent the night in their bed with the Kid.

A few months after the divorce was final she met Preston: a man who shared her preference for a life without highs and lows, a man who held a regular position which he adored, who seemed easily content with routine weekend sex and an occasional bottle of decent wine, who knew nothing about the cultural trends of modern life and who was so unlikeable, to most people, that it appeared unlikely he would ever form a relationship to threaten their own. Safe, reliable, stolid, uncomplicated Press, whom she soon came to adore without any need for passion, excitement, or keeping up with her old acquaintances. The little fellow had been so shy it was Angela herself who had to propose, and his swift acquiescence was so consumingly grateful that he stammered it out and didn't even ask to sleep with her until after they were married.

Lucy came along, in time, graced with her own good looks and with the simple needs and cooperative moods of both parents. Angela gave up interior decoration. Life was untainted;

memories slid into a burning little corner of her mind; and it remained just that placid and consolingly ordinary until they moved to Stevenson, Indiana, and met Cort Devalyn.

It was so damned *odd* about Cort. Outwardly, he was not only jovial and witty but crammed with knowledge. Even now, leaving Lucy in her room as she began another lonely evening in the front room of the new apartment, she had to admit that she didn't know why she disliked Cort so much. Angela doubted that she'd ever met a more intelligent or better educated man or one who was outwardly more considerate. But wasn't that part of the problem, really? She tried to imagine what the lean and lanky teacher needed from her husband—a man who singlemindedly had sought a career in dentistry and who, having achieved it, never cracked a book, followed politics, or did more than scan the newspaper. On *what*, Angela continued to wonder, was their alliance based?

The first inkling of trouble came when she learned that Press enjoyed hunting, something he'd never mentioned before. He even began to boast of his prowess, adding that he was "a natural psychologist of the living. I've been on the outside so much, I've had a chance to be detached and learn what makes things tick." The first quarrel they had developed when Press and the tall anthropology teacher returned from a Saturday outing and plunked down on her kitchen counter three exceedingly dead and swiftly hardening rabbits. With their tongues lolling from the corners of their mouths and their eyes forever fixed in fright. Angela felt she'd never seen anything more disgusting. And she was meant to skin and fry them. When the fuss began, she'd thrown Cort out of the apartment and seen, for the first time, the glint of unforgiving anger in his soft brown eyes.

Now she remembered how her husband, a good two inches shorter than she, stood toe-to-toe and shouted at her. "People have always told me no, Angela! All my early years I stopped doing things I really wanted to do because they made me feel so unwanted, so despicably meaningless. Try to *understand*, for God's sake!" he'd screamed. "Cort is the only really intelligent, worthwhile man who ever liked me, and he's a genuine genius! What's more, Angela, *he needs me*—he needs what I can give him, and that makes me feel important. Important, Angela, for the first time in my miserable, friendless existence! *Needed*, by someone I can respect!"

After that, well, she let Press spend as much time with Cort as he wished, always pleading to go along, always privately praying that it was no more than a friendship between the two men. Instead of banishing Cort, she'd tried to make friends with the teacher's blonde wife, Ellie—to change it into a foursome.

But it was only sweet Ginny Simmons who would tolerate Press long enough to form a relationship with Angela. The other women in the Knightsbury complex, including Ellie Devalyn, were polite but insisted on seeing her as an indivisible attachment to the dentist.

It was true that Cort sometimes came alone to dinner, dressed in his absurd checkered walking shorts even before summer arrived, and was unfailingly amiable and polite to her. She would see the unforgetting glint of insult deep in his eyes, however; and before the evening was out—whatever Angela did to strive to avoid it—there Cort would be, alone with Press in the den, huddled together . . . and *whispering*.

That was the first thing that really got on her nerves. The way she was excluded from their talks; the way they seemed, somehow, to be laying plans that had nothing whatever to do with hunting; the way they *whispered*, harshly and animatedly, Cort's angular face twisted in an expression of persuasion and Press' looking alternately ambivalently resistant and happily agreeable. Angela could remember how she'd stood just inside the apartment kitchenette, palms pressed against the wall, shamelessly eavesdropping—

—And the only clue she'd ever derived, to explain what was going on between the unlikely friends, was Press' plaintive query: *"You're certain they'll always like me?"* *"Certain,"* replied the teacher, firmly; and the last thing she heard from Press was a doubtful, *"Perhaps I should. Perhaps I should . . ."*

He'd refused, again, to explain what they were discussing. But just a couple of weeks ago, Press had turned to her in bed with a request: "I've looked at your X-rays again and I want you to come in this week for an extraction."

Angela remembered sitting up in bed, startled and resisting. She'd switched on the bedlamp and stared down at the dentist, burrowed like a mole beneath the covers, only his large oval head poking out to peer up at her nearsightedly. "I haven't had an ounce of pain in any of my teeth," she'd replied. "Not an ounce! Why should I have any of them pulled?"

"I *am* an oral surgeon, you know," Press had replied. "Trust me."

"The first time I have pain," she promised him, frowning and switching the light off.

"It should be done this week," he told her in the dark, his

palm heavy and firm on her bare shoulder. She remembered now that his breath had stank of garlic. "I won't hurt you."

"Not till I have pain," she'd said, lying on her side away from him. Peeved, she'd sighed and added, "Honestly, Press, sometimes I think you're going crazy."

He'd been silent a moment, then sighed heavily himself and muttered, in the summer-ponderous darkness of the apartment, "Maybe you're right."

Over the next few days he'd asked her, over and over. Cort had dropped by, full of charm and jokes about the hot weather, and Press had told his friend that Angela wouldn't let him pull "a bad tooth." Cort laughed in that superior way he had, sometimes, and chided her for her obvious foolishness. "Anyone married to a professional person should take advantage of his free services. After all, I'm sure Press knows what he's doing."

"Well, I'm not," she had retorted, "and I'm going to tell you one more time, *Professor* Devalyn, to keep your long nose out of my business."

Cort had left in a huff. There'd been another screaming match with Press. And two days later, exhausted from the demands and putting up with Cort's seemingly unnatural interest in Press' affairs, she'd left Press while he was at the office.

Days later she still didn't know exactly why she'd told no one but Ginny Simmons where she had taken little Lucy. She only knew that, since the moment Press mentioned her urgent need for an extraction, she'd been filled with a steadily-gathering, anxious conviction of dire risk. She'd come to feel that she was in more dangerous circumstances even than she'd known with Roger, her first husband, and she couldn't tolerate a replay, if it should come to that.

J. N. Williamson

Angela's plans were eventually to get back into interior decorating, but first there was the matter of rent. Yesterday she'd accepted a temporary job as assistant teller at the Stevenson First Bank & Trust. In her quietly determined, commonsense way, she'd figured she would have enough money saved up to strike out on her own again by the end of the year.

She was curled up on the front room couch, working her way through a foot-high stack of magazines that helped bring her up to date on current styles, when she heard the soft, almost secretive *tap-tap-tap* at the apartment door.

Angela dropped the magazine to the floor and looked across the room at the door, staring as if she might see through it. Her old reliable logic told her it had to be Ginny, who knew her whereabouts. But *this* knocking lacked the upfront here-I-am manner of her friend. It seemed surreptitious. Meant for her ears alone.

Barefoot and wearing only a robe over her underwear, Angela padded to the door and asked, without opening it, "Who is it?"

"I thought you might recognize my knock by now," a voice replied.

Angela blinked in surprise, then unlocked the door. She put her hands on her hips as she looked out into the quiet hallway. "Well, I sure didn't expect *you* to be here," she said.

"But I am," the caller replied, lightly, and an arm described an arc which ended at Angela's temple.

The blow drove her back into the apartment, staggering. She put up a hand as if to fend the attacker away; she stared in terror, too stunned to cry out; and then the object in the

THE DENTIST

caller's hand slashed across her forehead and, as she began to fall, collided heavily with the top of her head.

A new redness drenched her hair. Angela Sumner was dead before she hit the carpeted floor. A sticky pool formed beneath her skull, spreading with surprising evenness in all directions and matching the flecks of blood already staining the wall and door.

The visitor, hands gloved, closed the door, then knelt to feel for her pulse. There was none. Satisfied, one gloved hand lifted her head.

Moments later, the attacker straightened and looked down at the handkerchief cupped in one of the gloved hands.

Two white teeth gleamed there.

Carefully and neatly folded, the handkerchief disappeared into the pocket of the caller. He began purposely striding down the apartment hallway.

Toward the bedroom in which five-year-old Lucy Sumner was sound asleep.

At precisely the moment Angela was opening the door of her apartment for the final time, Alan Simmons was dealing a hand of pinochle.

"You're tough tonight, Press," he acknowledged to the small dentist. "Why, you haven't been set yet."

"That's because I never go for the widow," Press answered levelly, referring to the three cards left over when the game was played by three people. The one who made the high bid, to name trump, acquired them. "While it's possible to make your run or a double pinochle, you're statistically just as likely to draw something that eliminates a void suit or makes it impossible to make decent leads."

Ginny studied the dentist covertly as he retrieved his smouldering cigar from a littered ashtray. She thought, first, how hard it would be to get that damned stink out of the apartment; second, how Press seemed more sure of himself lately; third, how he wasn't really as ugly as she'd thought, that it was his miserable attitude at fault. "Most people don't have the self-control or patience to let the widow go, hand after hand," she observed.

"Thank you, Virginia," he replied with a flicker of an allowed smile. "If I have one thing in the world to brag about, it's my self-control. Discipline is one's best asset when he has a clear goal in mind—and I always do, eventually."

"Some people play games just for fun," Alan remarked, taking most of the sting out with a grin. "I wonder why Cort never showed up. Isn't he taking you home?"

Press looked at his wristwatch. "Why, yes, it's after eleven." He saw the Simmons boy, Luke, coming in the front door. "Well, there's Doctor IQ himself."

Luke glanced from his parents to the dentist and back again. He dropped his gaze and came toward the card table softly, almost deliberately. "Hi, everybody."

"Where have you been?" Ginny demanded, catching the nine-year-old by the hand and pulling him closer. "I was getting very worried about you."

"I was over at Brian's, just talking. He's really pretty neat, a smart guy himself." Something dark and unstated flickered behind his thick lenses. "You'd be amazed how he never misses a trick. He sees everything that goes on around him."

"I think you missed that trick, Alan," Press remarked, drawing in three cards. He looked back up at the boy, mild curiosity on his normally expressionless face. "You didn't

THE DENTIST

happen to see Uncle Cort, did you? We've been expecting him for two hours."

Luke paused, as if considering the question. "Why, no. Brian's smallest brother, Teddy, was there."

"I don't think you miss much either, Luke," the dentist murmured. "Especially after bringing up the Etruscans and pulling slaves' teeth the other night. Do you know how to play pinochle yet?"

"Mom and Dad taught me," Luke answered quickly, "but I thought it was kind-of a kids' game really."

He'd spoken so thoughtlessly but uncritically that all three adults burst into laughter.

"Be careful, pal," his father warned him, "or Uncle Press will rip your baby teeth out by the roots Wednesday." A sudden thought occured to him. He turned back to the card table, mildly puzzled. "Saturday night, at the clubhouse," he said ruminatively, "how come it wasn't *you* who mentioned the ancient Etruscans? You're such a fine oral surgeon I'd have thought you'd enjoy discussing the history."

"Not so," Press replied, blinking when the drifting smoke from his stogie smarted in his eyes. "I'm interested in neither ancient history nor theoretical possibility." A chunky finger poked beneath his glasses at his offended eye. "Now I'd not have been surprised if Cort brought it up. He *is* an anthropologist, remember. Perhaps I'm too practical for my own good."

The doorbell jangled and Alan rose to go. When the others saw who appeared in the doorway, they joined Alan there.

Cort Devalyn, skeletal and shrouded by night, smiled apologetically in at them. "I'm sure sorry we missed all the fun but we had car trouble on the way over." He thumbed

45

over his shoulder, indicating his late model Mustang. Alan saw a feminine figure, indistinct in the dark, seated in the front on the passenger side, and waved. "Ellie was so pissed by the delay and the expense of the repairs she didn't even want to come in." He nodded at the dentist. "I just stopped by to fetch Press."

The dentist nodded and took three steps way from the door. He turned, smiling at Alan and Ginny. "I enjoyed the game tonight. Thanks for having me."

The Simmon's stood arm-in-arm, affably waving as their two friends trotted back to the car. Luke stared, started down the walk toward the Mustang, then realized it was pulling away.

"I don't get it," the boy commented to his parents. "Uncle Cort said that *they* had car trouble—but Aunt Ellie was playing with the other kids when I was visiting Brian."

"They probably made a late start for some personal reason," Alan observed lightly, stepping back into the apartment after Ginny. "Cort probably came back for her, and then they came over here."

"I don't know," Ginny said doubtfully, looking up and making sure the door was tight in the frame. "I don't know about that at all."

Alan yawned, turned back to her and slipped his hands around her waist. "Now why in the world do you doubt that?" he asked her good-humoredly.

Ginny's lips tightened. "Because Ellie is a blonde," she replied on a note of anxiety. "And I'd swear that woman we saw in Cort's car was a redhead."

THREE

After sending Luke to bed and cleaning up, they walked lazily down the short hallway toward the triangular grouping of rooms at the back of the apartment—bath, little Luke's quarters, their own bedroom—and Alan held back. He wanted to be sure Luke was sound asleep behind his closed door.

In common with most other married couples who had children, Alan and Ginny always had to make certain the boy was deep in dreams before even entertaining the possibility of sharing sex. It was the one factor about having a son that seriously irritated Alan, so he listened grimly, perspiration from the humid night dark between his shoulder blades. Maybe it was plain childish of him, he mused again, but he really believed a man should be able to enjoy his wife whenever he wanted. If he hadn't, once, Luke wouldn't even be here.

It reminded his writer's mind of the first time he'd persuaded Ginny to go to bed with him, before they were married. Her sleeping parents had been in the next room, the old man raucously snoring, while Alan and Ginny quietly undressed each other and stretched out on the carpeted floor, using a sofa as a protective barrier. For him, it had been an ecstatic moment that convinced him he had to marry the young lady he'd dated since high school, but both of them had been obliged to struggle valiantly against making a noise. Now, he frowned. He'd traded two snoopy old strangers, acting as guardians of their daughter's rounded anatomy, for a nine-year-old boy whom he sometimes believed was nearly as much a stranger. He loved Luke, without question; but it was hard not to notice the boy's sharp differences from his own youth—the way Luke adored reading, and loved study even more, whereas Alan had liked an occasional book but delayed his studies to the last possible moment. Except for the fact that both father and son were fair to the point of appearing pale, he might have wondered if they had been given the wrong child to take home. That, and the three teeth in tiny Luke's mouth.

Tonight, however, there wasn't a sound from behind his door and Alan didn't believe Luke was the prying kind. Ginny, he saw, had gone on to the bathroom, so he entered their own room yawning, peeling off his shirt and pants. After a pause he removed his T-shirt as well. That was one of the key signals, to Ginny, that he'd like to make love.

The bedroom was simultaneously messy and entirely, even

The Dentist

gloriously comfortable. Mess in part because their first bedroom suite had begun to go, and the unmatching chair and dresser seemed incongruous; in part because Ginny was an indifferent housekeeper. She rarely made the bed until just before they retired. She permitted piles of their once-worn clothes to gather on a table against the wall, remembering to take it to the complex washer every few weeks. Comfortable, because he could relax and be himself here. Alan truly believed in the sanctity of a man's sleeping quarters, if not his entire house, and never permitted anyone but Ginny access to the room.

Whenever he had criticized Ginny for the way she let the apartment go, she was quick to flare up, her emerald eyes sparkling, eagerly pointing out that she, too, held a job. The fact that it was a part-time position was something Alan didn't dare voice. Privately, he understood Ginny was apathetic about keeping house because of a deepseated resentment for her autocratic and compulsive mother, whose place Alan referred to as "the poor man's Taj Mahal." When they'd made love on the carpet and afterward discovered a stain, the two young lovers spent two hours in the semi-darkness of the unlit front room, on their hands and knees, giggling softly as they strove to get the stain out. Mom, Ginny felt, was sure to notice; and she'd been correct. Until escaping to her own marriage with Alan, four months later, Ginny had been obliged to devise a dozen incredibly innovative guesses about the source of the stain. They went to the altar the day she finally ran out.

Alan sat on the edge of the bed, a rather thin man without his clothes, staring at the garments in the closet without seeing them. He was thinking, in his journalistic fashion, of how fascinating an institution marriage could be when one observed its progress. Alan preferred thinking of it that way; as progress, or development, something ongoing and forward-looking. Somewhat romantically he recalled the urgency he had once felt pounding and surging within him to see Ginny naked, to touch and kiss those warm, secret parts of her body which social propriety had prevented him from seeing. Their honeymoon, in neighboring Cincinnati, hadn't been at all spoiled by that earlier sharing of their bodies; it had been the most thrilling week of Alan's young life.

But it also marked the gradual transition to the next stage of their relationship. Familiar with the way she looked, after a few months of marriage, there had been the new joy of greater control and the opportunity to explore the breadth and depth of intercourse. Strangely, he supposed, Alan had never looked at what he and Ginny did together as dirty in any sense of the word. If it had been acceptable, he guessed, he might have told everyone he knew what they did and how much they enjoyed it—in a good-humored recommendation to his bachelor friends of the institution they kept so gingerly at bay. For two or three years he had been as diligent in learning fresh ways to love his wife as he was in learning the newspaper business.

Now, it seemed to Alan as he looked up to see Ginny enter the bedroom, without clothes, they were probably entering a new stage. Sex was less frequent now, although no less fulfilling from his standpoint; and the odd thing was that having relations with Ginny only once a week or so made the *quality* of their time together even better.

He gave her a lopsided grin as she came round the edge of the bed to stand in front of him. "How'd you know I wanted to do it tonight?" he asked. She usually wore a nightgown to bed.

"I could be a genius," she said snappily, smiling down at him, "or maybe I just noticed your imitation of a hound-dog outside Luke's room. If you want to be that careful, Alan, we could save up for a TV camera to be mounted on his wall. That way, we'd know for sure whether he was asleep or not."

He pulled her belly against his face, his fingers gently trailing the faint stretchmarks and marveling again at the yielding softness of his wife. "Hell, darlin', that's exactly what I'm afraid *Luke* is doing!" He laughed and moved his hands lower. "Do you think we ought to examine the room for bugs?"

"I think we should examine other matters entirely," she whispered, abruptly excited and pulling away to drop to the bed. Her arms reached up to him.

He knelt on the bed as she tugged his shorts down, then cupped his erection in gentle fingers. Alan moaned, kicked the shorts to the floor, and reclined beside her. "I want you so much," he groaned, already lifting himself tentatively above her and staring at the expanse of beauty beneath him. "So much."

Ginny smiled fondly and drew him down. "That's what I'm here for."

Later, satisfied, she thought of insisting that she had been right—that the woman in Cort's car was redhaired, not blonde like Ellie. Alan had thought it was the lighting. Now he was beside her, as warm and relaxed as a contented puppy beside a fire. Clearly enough, she surely *was* wrong. He was probably right. Had Press not been there, too, she might have considered it possible that Cort was with another woman; but even though the two men were close, it was hard to believe the teacher would flaunt his adultery before the dentist. Ginny sighed, curled up around Alan's now slumbering back, and tried to go to sleep.

She didn't succeed, however, until more than sixty cat-footed minutes had tiptoed stealthily past and she was shivering, despite the night's humidity, in the dark. Not that it was something she was ready to bring up to Alan; but Ginny couldn't keep from feeling that there was something peculiarly . . . *sinister* . . . going on, something alarming happening, in their little circle of companions.

It was especially hard to sleep when she remembered that, while Ellie was, indeed, a blonde, Press' separated wife had red hair. Was there the slightest lunatic possibility that the woman she'd seen in Cort's car was actually Angela Sumner?

"Yes, yes!" the tall man shouted, quite oblivious to the four children sleeping elsewhere in the apartment. His arms stretched out, skin taut, muscles bunched, hands clenching and unclenching. "*Now*, Ellie, *now!*"

Ellie slid back and forth as fast as she could, even though he was strangely cold in her, cold and impossibly rockhard. Her eyes, gazing down at Cort, were nearly frightened. His face was contorted in a paroxym of passion. Even his gums showed in the terrible expression. Cort hadn't displayed so much urgency for sex for over two years and now, she thought with a mixture of surprised and half-formed concern, it was as though all his old needs had been rekindled. Unnaturally aroused.

His hips shot up from the bed, lifting the plump blonde with him; his long fingers clawed at her chunky breasts,

The Dentist

locking hurtingly on them; his penetration went deep as he exploded into her—

—And then Ellie was sinking onto him, impaled, her hair spreading across her round face and hiding Cort's. Slowly, drainingly, the anthropology teacher finished and subsided. His arms collapsed against the mattress, and his breath came for another minute in heavy pants.

It had been like ice, she thought. "W-Was it okay?" she asked softly. She would have found it impossible to explain why the question came out stammeringly, timorously. He'd never been a brutal man; he'd never laid a hand on her.

But the truth was that Cort Devalyn made her just a little afraid, these days, and she feared to her soul that she knew the general explanation for it: Cort was changing, again.

And if he was changing back, *all the way back*, she might have to rethink her old conclusions.

Reevaluate the decision she'd reached before agreeing to marry him, that there was nothing to the concept of "the sins of the fathers" and her other, old conviction that there was really no such thing as "evil." Only painful memories of a cruel early upbringing that had left vicious scars on the psyche.

Cort fell asleep. It was so swift even Ellie was surprised. She had barely dismounted and begun moving toward the bathroom when his high, tenor, whining snore followed her like a persistent shadow.

Completing her ablutions, Ellie slipped into a robe. She noticed that it barely went round her middle, although it was only a year old, and she paused to stand on the bathroom scales: 146 pounds, the most she'd weighed since high school. High school, when she'd experienced the wonderful thrill of being wanted by the most brilliant boy in the senior class. Cort himself, president of the class, a straight-A student, the one they said had the brightest future of all the kids graduating from Stevenson High. He told her he preferred women "with a little meat on their bones," added with that wit's charm of his that he "liked girls he could hold onto" when they did it. Because he'd been the only boy in high school who ever wanted to date her, it seemed entirely natural that they marry and that she give him four healthy, wonderful children in eight years.

She went out to the small alcove between the front room and the dining room. There, Ellie had set up a permanent card table for her astrological materials: blank horoscope sheets; a good atlas; note paper for calculations; and a number of odd little leatherbound books called *ephemeride*. In the latter, the positions of the sun, moon, and all the planets in this solar system were indicated by sign and degree, for all the years back to 1800 and reaching to the Twenty-First Century.

Although the lighting was poor in the alcove, it was comforting to Ellie to sit at this table—hers—reassuring to pull out the two-inch-thick stack of completed horoscopes representing the characters of Cort, their kids, and all their friends. A lot of know-it-all people thought she was a trifle strange for putting such stock in astrology. But blonde Ellie knew astrology was the oldest organized subject, or discipline, on the face of the earth, and she believed that any errors cropping up were those of the practitioner—*not* of astrology. She saw astrology as an unbelievably exotic love-partner slow to reveal itself, and as a field of study at least as complex as anything scientific types like Cort subscribed to.

The Dentist

Amusing, conflicted, sometimes-sweet, blissfully forgetful Cort. Back when they pledged themselves to one another but before the formality of marriage, Ellie had laughed at the idea that he might be anything like his madman father. When, as a freshman in college, he sometimes did antisocial things ranging from teenage pranks to actions that could have imprisoned him for a year or more, and he claimed fearfully that he was becoming "just like my old man," Ellie's honest amusement—a refusal to take his deeds seriously—brought him quickly back to normal behavior. Once, enlisting her father's help, she even got him out of trouble and had the wise good graces never to remind him of the occasion.

When the day came to be married, Cort ran naked through the neighborhood after making love to her, his head thrown back and howling like a dog. He'd promised to kill someone "as a sacrifice to my father," but he hadn't; and when Ellie told the amused policeman who brought Cort back that he was on his honeymoon, the officer left him with her.

"It's all astrology, babe," she told him that night when he was himself again. "Your real-life father was a Scorpio and you're an Aquarian. The combination of Pluto- and Uranus-ruled signs causes people to bite off more than they can chew, and sometimes the stress becomes too much. Remember, Cort: evil doesn't exist. We're all biomagnetic creatures operated by mechanisms, like machines—the mechanisms of the heavens; the aspects formed by the planets."

Cort had asked her, curious then as he leaned on his elbow in their honeymoon bed, "What was my old man's horoscope like?"

"Brilliant," she'd told him, and then shuddered. "But *diabolical*. Machiavellian."

Two years of marriage had passed before the change occurred, before something extraordinary—and blessed, Ellie felt in an uncharacteristic burst of religious zeal—happened to her Cort:

An odd but beneficial mental block slipped into place in youthful Cort Devalyn's mind, almost like something that dissociated the two hemispheres of his brain. He still remembered that his real name was Bellefontaine, that he'd killed his unmarried mother simply by being born, that he'd been the offspring of a powerful and gifted but apparently evil man, and that he'd actually been reared by an elderly couple named Bonnabelle and Louis Devalyn. But somehow he *forgot*, totally, all details concerning his real father.

It was as if the elder Bellefontaine had never existed. Cort could not even recall what the old man had *been* or what he had *done*. Ellie remembered, with fear and disgust, but she wasn't about to remind Cort. Soon he was able to speak of the lapse in his memory and claimed that he was like a man who'd had a nervous breakdown but remembered, afterward, little of what occurred. At last, he'd told Ellie with genuine joy, he could be free enough of the Bellefontaine traces to build a respectable career and happy family without being hampered by a past that was, after all, none of his fault.

All those things Cort had done, and more. But now, Ellie could see both in his behavior and in his concentrated horoscope, he was again changing—back, perhaps, to the man who once experienced moments of imminent madness, and who had believed with psychic anguish that he was capable of blind, unheeding violence.

Ellie lifted a certain horoscope paper, inserted the upcom-

THE DENTIST

ing transit of Mars in the cardinal-water sign Cancer, and the tip of her pencil broke beneath the pressure she was applying. "Shit!" she growled, staring at it. Despite the hot night, she shivered and drew the robe tight around her breast, like a sorcerer or necromancer a thousand years before. That damned Preston Sumner, *he* was the catalyst of this! It was hard to say how, but the friendship he'd formed with Cort surely started it! Why, a beginner in astrology or even in psychology could recognize it at once!

Press was a dedicated but stubborn, career-minded Capricorn with his moon in vain, look-at-me Leo. His natal Seventh House was presently afflicted by Mars, clear evidence (to Ellie Devalyn) of unwise new partnership interests. Interests affecting the family circle, and one's person. Besides, Ellie ruminated, Capricorn preceded Aquarius; and while it didn't hold the authority or dominance of an upper square, it did *use* electrically changeable and inventive Aquarius, the way some calloused old leches used young women. It would surely take a true act of will on Cort's part to escape the mutual influences they shared and to realize to what an extent, plain, unattractive, outwardly harmless Press Sumner was using him for his own secret purposes.

Not that it was entirely a one-way street, she confessed to herself, holding the paper below the light of her lamp. Cort's Mercury was in Capricorn, just as was Press'. It suggested that some persons, like Press, could be such blank slates, such dim personalities, that a brilliant man like Cort could not resist *writing* on them—even when he didn't realize that he, too, was being manipulated. And right now, in troubled Ellie Devalyn's view, some potentially terrible and frightening message was being scrawled on the blackboard.

Unbeckoned, a thought occurred to her, poking up from her unconscious mind like some wildly malicious weed determined to surface: If Cort was again becoming peculiar and inherently dangerous, was his forgetful "nervous breakdown" *getting well?* Was he merely returning to his own bizarre and frightening personal "normal?"

Which personality—the former half-addled, haunted, perverse one or the newer kind, studious, clever and decent one—was the *real* Cort Devalyn?

He was tall for his tender years. His arms and legs stuck out from his body like broken things with a life of their own, a study in boyish geometry. Cort saw him there clearly, almost as if he'd been awake; but it took his sleeping mind another timeless instant to realize that it was young Cort Bellefontaine whom he was watching: himself.

Then he began to see from the young boy's eyes, in the way of certain nightmares—a magical out-of-body experience that snapped him suddenly into his own two-year-old head, returning him to a life of largely forgotten pain and confusion.

The impressive figure high above him was costumed in a tuxedo and a floor-length black cape that rose, bat-like, round the back of his enormous head, coming to a sharp and imposing point on the forehead. He could not see the face clearly except for the agate eyes that glowed with the fiercest kind of intensity. Most of the face was in shadow, whether in Cort's dream or at the time the event occurred in his youth; but he knew without question that this menacing figure was his own father. What was he doing? Why was he, himself, unable to move?

A sound, nightmare-conceived or recalled. The two pair of

THE DENTIST

eyes—Cort-*past*; Cort-*present*—turned to See. His gaze swept restlessly, fearfully, past several burning candles to a number of women of varying ages. Each was naked except for a black hood that covered the entire skull, the hair drawn beneath it so that an impression of hairlessness—even sexlessness—was created despite the bobbing breasts. They drifted round and round the table to which he was strapped and, as they passed Cort's lower portions—the realization of his own bareness shocked both Cort-*past* and Cort-*present*—they dribbled from ornate bottles some pungent-smelling globules that seemed to freeze and confine him from the small waist down. When the bizarre women began almost to race in soundless circles, dizzying him and leaving him nauseated, the two Corts looked back at the male figure towering over their head.

The shadow—the ominous figure—the man who was surely his own, real father—drew from the privately voluminous womb of his sweeping cape a gleaming and immense knife. Both Corts shrank from it in terror. It resembled a short sword; it had a scarab glittering in the base of the hilt like a single Cyclopean eye. It mesmerized the Corts, easily gripped their dimming minds in an obscene caress that made the boy and man tremble in a fright remembered only in the depths of racial consciousness—a counsciousness that husbanded within its timeless, dark self, secrets no man wished to confront.

Crashing sounds then . . . Other faces, dimly seen through the haze of time . . . Sturdy adult men wearing the same kind of clothing . . . Screams and snarls from the hood-headed, bare-bodied women who cowered, hissing like tigresses, against the far wall . . . An image of ghastly, almost unthinkable resistance and a swift last effort to harm the boy-Cort on the part of the caped and beshadowed figure, who was—

Who was . . . *whom?*

Cort, the sleeping Cort, opened his horror-struck eyes. He stared into the murky pockets of night without finding the change of salvation. Ellie, he found when he groped for her, afraid, was gone from their bed. A beshadowed figure in a cape who was—he asked himself again, squinting in fleeting concentration against the friendly enmity of the longer night—*whom?*

He could not recall. The nightmare receded like the light of a television that had been shut off. Perspiring heavily, the teacher perched on the edge of the bed and, when the idea came to him, he could not know whether it was right or not.

But it seemed possible to Cort that he'd had a nightmare about Preston Sumner, his good friend—his new partner in an undertaking they could not discuss with a living soul. Press, the dentist.

FOUR

The Tuesday before the Wednesday in late July when the Simmons and Devalyn families were scheduled to visit him, Doctor Preston Sumner spent the morning creating pain.

Stocky and strong, young enough to be in trim and certainly dedicated to his work, Doctor Sumner toiled that morning like a man possessed. Perhaps he was, if it came down to that. One or two of those who staggered away from his surgery, holding on to their painracked jaws with both hands, knew that there had to be *some* explanation for the way Preston Sumner had lost all his flair for holding pain at bay.

But the special effectiveness of the man involved with evil is that no one else knows about the commitment, not enough to troop to the police department and file a complaint. Better to think that the blood flowing Tuesday morning in tiny Stevenson was the work of a hangover, say, disturbing the good doctor—a sudden need for better spectacles, perhaps, or a severe case of overwork.

None of his patients suspected the truth and, if they had been told it by the dentist himself, they might not have believed him.

Simply, Press Sumner hadn't been informed as yet of what *precisely* was required in order to achieve his terrible, private goals. He had going for him, fundamentally, three things at best: the knowledge that pain must be created at his own malicious hands; the experience that people who knew nothing of his science would willingly subject themselves to his cruelty; and the absolute belief that he could accomplish what he sought by mercilessly digging into mouth after mouth, probing with wide-eyed abandon into tender gums and shrieking cavities.

Earlier, it had been hard for him. It had seemed then to be a conscious violation of a sacred oath, a contradiction of all the skills he had so assiduously developed.

But by midmorning Tuesday, the truth was that Press didn't care any longer. Blinded by his determination to fulfill personal objectives at any cost, he went at each person naively waiting in his chair with a kind of manic creative inspiration. Each of them was going to lose at least one tooth, another fact none of them was privy to, and to handle as many patients as possible, Press moved with harsh, vulpine speed. It no longer mattered to him whether the extracted teeth were diseased or infected, although it occurred to him, at one

The Dentist

point, to hope they were not. Unquestionably healthy teeth would be vastly more useful to the Plan.

When somewhat over three hours had passed, and the dentist's schedule cleared for lunch, Preston Sumner chose and lit a foul cigar, then stood trembling at the front door of his waiting room with a vaguely disturbing feeling of being haunted. If teeth possessed souls, his was a mass murder that surely demanded vengeance—and he knew that his crime would continue until he had all the information he needed, or until no more patients returned. Hands and arms aching from the morning's effort, Sumner half-expected to see a band of torch-bearing townfolk gathering on his stoop like the furious people milling before Castle Frankenstein. But that couldn't matter, not really; for in a pristine, plastic container in the back, he had collected the largest number of teeth he'd ever managed in a week—let alone a single morning.

He heard his private telephone jangling in the tiny room behind the surgery and, knowing how few people even knew the number existed, trotted back to it with alacrity. His forehead at once cold and flushed with perspiration, he snatched the phone out of its box-like container and barked into it: "Who is this?"

"Let's not waste time, you know who," the voice replied with acerbity. "Listen closely. *I have the answers.*"

The dentist felt faint. Sumner, whom many people at dental college used to say resembled a frog, even at his best moments, found his eyes fairly popping from their head. *"Tell me,"* he whispered with a degree of urgency uncharacteristic of his phlegmatic personality. "What kind of people do we actually require?"

For a full five minutes the bulldog of a dentist listened

attentively to the complex, arcane explanation. There would be no backing out now. Anything that was needed—*whatever* had to be done—had just become acceptable. His gaze was fixed, beyond the window, on an alley behind the office. A tawny, starved-looking cat had vaulted to the wooden fence with some ghoulish prize won from a nearby garbage can. The can still rolled on the ground, dripping things.

But Press didn't actually see the animal. His thoughts were fixed on the incredible fact that their recent enterprises hadn't been exercises but genuine scientific fact-finding, that there really *was* a way he could have all those things he'd always sought, more than anything else in the world. Like the feline on the fence, he chewed the data in his mind and found only one scrap of knowledge hard to digest.

"Why does it have to be *them*?" he asked. The reply was snapped into his ear like a mousetrap going off. Delicately, he held the phone slightly away from his ear. "Yes, yes, I do see, of course. It just seems a pity that it has to be them." Again he listened to the reprimand, grimacing. "I understand there can be no room for weakness when everything lies just ahead. But let me have the afternoon to try a few more, all right? It's a pity to see this morning's exhausting work go for nothing. You can run tests on today's bunch and there'll still be time before tomorrow."

When he had his way and replaced the receiver in its stylish cradle, Doc Sumner relit his cigar and smiled with satisfaction. He'd be able to do the decent thing, one last time. Try to find somebody else who qualified—strangers who would fit the bill.

Then, if it wouldn't work any other way, he would simply have to go after the families of Alan Simmons and Cort Devalyn.

The Dentist

* * *

Ginny had Alan's lunch ready for him when he came home. She'd felt sluggish lately, a little sapped by the hot weather. After she kissed him and put two Vienna sausage sandwiches and a tall glass of two-percent milk under his nose, she draped herself on his shoulders.

"I was wondering," she murmured, tickling the back of his neck, "if you could take a longer lunch hour tomorrow. We haven't eaten out in ages and it would be nice to drive into Indianapolis to Duff's, over on Shadeland." The restaurant had the lowest prices in town and all you wanted to eat at a fixed price. As a rule, when she included economical Duff's in her plea, he gave in. "You could tell Ernie that you're covering some little league game or something."

"Only one problem, darlin'," he replied over his shoulder. "Tomorrow's Wednesday."

Her brows arched. "You say it like it was Christmas."

"I said it like it was D-Day. D as in dentist," Alan said, taking a huge bite of his first sandwich. He talked around it, barely decipherable. "Press is expecting us."

"Shit," Ginny swore succinctly and moved away from him to take a seat on the other side of the table. She poured the remainder of her Diet Pepsi into a glass and frowned her annoyance. Ginny was a relatively stoic person where pain was concerned but hated having her rare impulses foiled.

Young Luke, who was plodding manfully through a bologna-and-cheese sandwich, actually brightened. "That's when you're taking me, huh? Tomorrow? When I get to see what Uncle Press does?"

Alan nodded and pursed his lips. "You won't be so darned anxious to go once you've been there a few times," he announced warningly. "For all I know, he may want to extract those baby teeth of yours. You have to have room for the permanent ones to come in."

"That's okay," Luke said, but there was a noticeable dimunition of enthusiasm. He set the sandwich back on its saucer and used his thumb and index finger to make one of his teeth wobble. "T'tell the truth, they been hurtin' a little lately anyhow."

"Luke, stop that!" Ginny snapped, turning away from the wriggly-tooth act with a comical shudder. "That looks positively awful!"

"I think," Luke began ignoring his mother, "I think maybe I'll be a dentist like Uncle Press when I grow up." He looked to each parent with brightly shining eyes. "It sounds interestin' and besides, you said dentists make a lot of dough."

Alan chuckled and reached over to rumple Luke's hair with affection. He gave a marveling smile to this little stranger who was always so different from him. "That figures," he remarked. "It really figures."

Tuesday was the day tall and slender Cort Devalyn taught summer school at Von Braun High, the building within walking distance of the Knightsbury apartment complex. Finished with his anthropology classes for the day, he returned to his private office on the second floor and sank into the chair at his desk.

The man's stork-like legs beneath the customary neat walking shorts presented something of a contrast to the Spartan appearance of the office. While Von Braun's principal allowed the faculty a great deal of latitude, in the hope of engendering a college-style atmosphere both for the teachers and the bright children who were enrolled there, Cort was such a serious instructor that he eschewed the paintings, posters, and bars of his fellow faculty members. His only departure from austerity was that he'd filled the built-in bookshelves both with volumes used in his classes and a rich variety of books of particular interest to him.

He had taken two of the latter from the shelf before sitting in a pool of warm sunlight streaming through the window behind him. He opened one of the books now, trying again to ignore the blinding headache. It seemed to cut from one temple to the other, writhing its distracting way directly across his *corpus callosum*, and he supposed he should see a physician about it. But a doctor would want a complete history. A doctor asked a lot of questions. And a doctor was not that distant from a psychiatrist. Years ago, he'd been obliged to endure questions from a whole battery of such men, and the very thought of putting himself in their hands again terrified Cort.

Who could tell what answers they might elicit from him?

Abruptly, the open book in front of him faded, the printed letters blurring. The lanky teacher clutched the edges of his desk desperately, knowing what was about to happen. It had, this past six weeks, several times. For an instant he tried to thrust the unwanted memory away. He concentrated on harmless, current matters, tried to visualize Ellie or his four children. But on the memory came, pounding in his skull like kettle drums, slowly but surely taking form as an image on the spread pages of the book even as the words that had been growled at him so long ago sounded in his shrinking ears as if the speaker sat across the desk from him.

A tall, powerfully-muscled man stood in front of a

small, thin boy perched nervously on the edge of a bed. He towered so far above the seated boy that his face was shadowed, and the boy fixed his gaze upon the enormous, costly ring which the man—surely his father—wore on the fourth finger of his left hand. It was a magnificent, sparkling object that the lad coveted. He found the ring hypnotic, at times soothing and yet oddly uplifting. For a moment he was not even capable of hearing the strong man, as he gaped openly at the ring on his finger.

At the pinnacle of the ring-face was the name Ra. At the base, he saw the word Geb. Young Cort knew that they meant "creator" and "earth." Between them he read the word Nut, or "sky." But the ring had twelve equal facets, a fact that intrigued the youth. He understood that the number Twelve represented the afterworld—a living afterworld in which one might cross the River Styx, or might be left behind to haunt the visible living.

Grown Cort, seeing the image with the clarity of a television screen, saw that the initials NTR were the most imposing feature of the great ring. They were spread prominently but in contrasting, emerald letters across the object's surface. For a moment, he could not remember what "NTR" meant and then, suddenly, he did: They stood for "divine being"—or one who watches. And the grown Cort recalled with a shudder both that this definition was also that of the ancient world's most advanced and gifted nation, Sumer, and that it could only be worn or used by the highest class of priesthood.

"We are different, my son," intoned the powerful man from his Olympian height. "Different because our family chose to be different, to probe for the wisdom of the ages. Our commitment, and our extraordinary abilities, are passed to the youngest son whether he desires them or not. Those in the afterworld will have it no

THE DENTIST

other way, my son. It is the obligation—the payment—each Bellefontaine must pay, to obey when one who watches speaks. Learn that, my son; know that it is true, and inescapable." For the first time, father's face became visible as the tall man stooped to the boy. The adult Cort saw the dark shadows melt away like black tallow from a burning candle. He cried out in shock and dismay, staring at the image. Except that he wore no glasses, Georges Bellefontaine's face was Cort's—but a Cort whose soft, brown eyes had become hot with lust, with manic need, commanding and utterly mad. Father's sensual lips parted: *"The message may come at any time, in any of numerous ways. But you must do its bidding, young Bellefontaine, even when it demands . . . the ultimate sacrifice."*

A dazzling flash of light seared the adult Cort's eyes. Pain burned his temples, his brain, even his teeth, and he cried out once more, throwing his fingers before his face.

When he dared take them tremblingly away, the book on the teacher's desk was only a book. Numb, he read where his gaze fell: "Zoser was a king of the Third Dynasty who lies now in the Step Pyramid at Sakkara, erected by the king's minister Imhotep. Imhotep may also have been history's first dentist. The Step is the oldest of all the pyramids, a giant edifice surrounded by a complex of buildings and a stone wall. There are those who continue to claim that the wall is not meant to keep strangers *out* but to keep mad Zoser *in*."

Cort blinked, lifted his head and stared out the window. Two teenagers were walking by, hand-in-hand. The normality of the scene was incongruous with what had happened. Now Cort knew why he had always been enthralled by studying ancient Egypt. He knew why it was his private passion, something he'd never shared with anyone, even sweet, understanding Ellie. That ring on Georges Bellefontaine's hand—glittering from the finger which generally indicated marriage, or one's closest attachment—bore *Egyptian* symbols! It spoke of what the Egyptians of old accepted as articles of truth! *Great God,* Cort thought with rising panic, *even when I've felt that I was most truly myself, and healthiest, I have merely been following in my father's footsteps.*

In a drawer of his desk he found an old, mangled pack of camels, pulled one out and, with some difficulty, lit it with his desk lighter. The stale smoke scalded his throat, left it raw; and as he coughed, Cort thought again of the terrible headaches. The latest was gone. When the vision, the awful memory of his clouded boyhood, ceased, so did the piercing headache.

It was all becoming clear. He let smoke filter through his nostrils; he really must kick the habit. The room appeared to darken slightly. These moments of absolute recall—these flashbacks—were the messages George Bellefontaine had told him he would someday receive. Just as clearly, he thought with fear, these messages came from his own father—a man who was now, himself, *one who watches.* A spirit in the afterworld. Clearly, the headaches would go away only when he did what he was being asked to do—when he stopped waffling and fully implemented his marvelous plan.

Cort's head bobbed in intense agreement with his thought. How he would adore telling Ellie, sharing the wonderful plan with her! But of course, she would never understand and, worse, it might be Ellie who had to be sacrificed. Unthinkable as it was, the choices might narrow down to the only human being who had ever truly loved him.

Thunder rolled in the skies above Von Braun High School

The Dentist

and Cort abruptly found himself seated in partial darkness. Lightning cracked at the window. Cort opened his desk drawer and tossed the cigarette pack into it. Then he paused; there were *other* things in the drawer. He squinted down at them. . . .

There was a crumbling, ancient papyrus under plastic protection. It bore the image of a thin, jet-black cat with a staring human face. Below the cat was a drawing of two bricks terminating in a human head. The cat represented Meshkent, the Egyptian goddess associated with childbirth, whose name meant "the place where one delivers." The inscription beneath it depicted the way Egyptian mothers crouched, when giving birth, supporting themselves on two bricks.

And beside the covered papyrus, in a small plastic container of their own, were two bloodied teeth from an adult human head.

Today, he realized, modern man tended to believe in nothing but birth and death. A dead-end cycle of pointlessness. Smug and essentially ignorant, man was inclined to run from the very mention of the word "death" and, where birth was concerned, often annihilated life before it even grew visible.

But for those people the anthropology teacher admired, the ancient civilization to which Bellefontaines were unalterably committed, there was instead a triad of life: birth, death, the afterlife. No educated Egyptian of old ever doubted for a moment that he would, one way or the other, continue existing . . . forever.

And the papyrus in his desk informed Cort that no intelligent Egyptian believed there was anything more symbolic of rich opportunity or more clearly indicative of the means to acquire what one pursued than the startling sight of teeth grinning in the mouth of a newborn child. They were not enough, alone, to hurtle all the barriers to success, no; but they were indispensable. In fact, nothing could be done without the proper teeth. In Heliopolis and elsewhere, dying Egyptian pharaohs participated in a ritual called "the opening of the mouth." Cort's papyrus revealed that if the teeth were of the proper kind and configuration, and if they were properly extracted, the pharaohs were quickly transported from the *yad*, or temple, to the divine abode of eternal Life. To dwell forever with *Ra*.

A newborn's teeth marked the genuine beginning of the path to success, if one was bold and brave enough to follow that path despite the likely cost.

A bolt of lightning shimmered at the office window, and Cort's face was caught in an expression of complete conviction. He did not know that, just then, his face was like that of his father Georges Bellefontaine. Now, he knew what had to be done; there could be no more delay for sentimental reasons. Not if his own secret plan was to come to reality.

It was all right, then, if he was following with unknowing obedience in his father's footsteps, even if his memory had not yet told precisely what the man was or had done in life.

But Cort could not help but wonder, as he turned on his high-intensity lamp with a shaking hand, in whose footsteps Georges Bellefontaine had followed.

FIVE

It was a beautiful, summery day in Stevenson, Indiana, but the inquisition was being reenacted in the oral surgeon's office.

Young Brian Devalyn was the last of the four children to be treated that Wednesday morning. All had been brought to the oral surgeon's office, along with their mother Ellie, in Alan and Ginny Simmons' car. Cort Devalyn, their father, had mentioned a faculty meeting at Von Braun High School while Ellie had acquired three driving tickets and didn't want to be behind the wheel for awhile. The two babies of the Devalyn family had been angels. Only Brian's immediately younger sister, twelve-year-old Laura, had complained; her pain had been so bad that Ginny volunteered to drive her home.

Now it was Brian's turn. Closing his eyes, he pressed his head as far back against the dentist chair as he possibly could, and then there was no escape.

"Does it hurt," inquired stocky Preston Sumner, *"here?"* His instrument prodded.

"No," Brian lied, mumbling. He felt as if his mouth contained two doubled fists and perhaps a pony or two. *Things* extruded from it like hospital tubes feeding a fatally-ill patient. "S'fine, Uncle Press."

"Really." A pause. "How about *here?*" Another jab.

Sweat broke out on the forehead of the fourteen-year-old. "No," he got the word out, tears leaping to his eyes. "Noddabid."

Sumner got a firm grip and jabbed harder. The instrument poked on through. A tiny jewel of scarlet blood took form inside the boy's mouth. The man grinned. "What about *here?*"

Brian shrieked. A bright-red shield of agony leapt before his outraged vision and spread, like running gore. Pain came to life in every inch of his jaw and skull like some bursting beast that had been lurking there all the time. Brian's hand came up to his cheek but Doc Sumner firmly batted it away.

"Well, I guess I got my little answer," the dentist murmured, laughing. He clapped Brian on the shoulder, and the pain rattled around in Brian's head like jagged pieces of internal shrapnel. "Hurt like hell, didn't it?"

Misery has a way of bringing out the truth in people. "Oh, yeah," the boy nodded, trying to clear his eyes of tears. The crimson haze lowered and he stared at the short man in white

THE DENTIST

before him, his feelings nearly as hurt as his gum. "But I don't think it's anything serious."

"Wrong." Press Sumner waggled a finger and looked cheerful. "Wrong, wrong, wrong! *That* one has to come out. Maybe the one next to it, too." He gestured to the bulbous-breasted brunette nearby. "Give us a hand with the gas, Nurse Crawford. We don't want this young man struggling and hurting himself."

Looking bored, Nurse Crawford did her thing. Last week she had replaced the middle-aged woman who'd been Doc Sumner's assistant for several years. She wasn't about to rock the new-employee boat.

Moments later, when Brian Devalyn was under, two strange things happened:

Another man, standing just inside Sumner's private room at the back, dried his eyes on a handkerchief.

And Doctor Preston Sumner leaned forward until his thick lips were within an inch of the fourteen-year-old's ear as he whispered, insistently: "Tell me what you *see*, Brian. Look *ahead*, boy; tell me what you *see*!"

Meanwhile, Alan Simmons and his son Luke sat by themselves in the waiting room. The newspaper reporter smiled shakily at to the boy when young Brian's screams penetrated the room. "There must be some problem. Brian is probably being a big sissy," Alan said without conviction.

"No." Luke shook his head stubbornly. Alan had never seen the boy so pale. "No way, dad, 'cause Brian's the bravest guy I know. Nothin' gets to him." He hesitated and bit his lower lip. "Usually."

"Well, I'm sure there's a good reason for all that commotion,"

Alan replied. "Don't you imagine Uncle Press accidentally hit a nerve?"

Luke didn't reply. He had just found that he couldn't move his gaze from the polished door leading to the interior of the dentist's office where, it began to seem to Luke, his ultimate fate awaited him. Despite his best effort to persuade himself otherwise, Luke's baby teeth were being so crowded by the permanent teeth struggling to emerge that he'd been in considerable discomfort for over two days. Until now, this last minute, he'd looked forward both to the educational experience of watching the teeth pulled and to the relief he was certain to feel. After all, doctors and dentists helped people.

Luke wasn't so sure anymore about any of it.

"D'you still want to be a dentist when you grow up?" Alan asked, trying to distract the boy.

For a moment there was no answer. Then, grudgingly, Luke's chin moved in a nod. "You're probably right, dad. Uncle Press must have just hit a nerve. Right?"

Alan nodded reassuringly back. "Right! Absolutely!"

Moments later, Brian came from the surgery with his left cheek puffy and his eyes red. He held a cold icebag against the offended area. To Luke, Brian looked as if his face had turned to cotton candy. Or marshmallow. "Where's Mom and Aunt Ginny?"

"Laura was in such pain, my wife took her back to your apartment," Alan answered. "Your mom went along. They'll both be back to pick you up."

"Sweep up the pieces, you mean," Brian moaned, plunking himself down in a chair to wait. He glared at the door

THE DENTIST

leading to the back. "The first time I went must have been a con, to get me back again. It wasn't half that bad before."

Nurse Crawford materialized in the doorway like a beautiful Popsicle. "The doctor is ready to see you, Mr. Simmons," she announced.

" 'See' as in 'total,' " Brian warned as Alan rose. "I think Uncle Press ruined me. I feel like there isn't a tooth left in my head. I'm completely hollowed-out!"

Alan grinned with more confidence than he felt and followed Nurse Crawford's heavily-starched white uniform. The reporter remembered an s-f story he'd read, years ago, about a man who thought he was going to the doctor but was really in a waiting room in hell. When he recalled the tale, he blanched and made his mind change the subject.

Press Sumner's greeting was cordial if somewhat guarded, Alan thought. Perhaps the balding little man was uneasy, meeting his friends in this milieu. When the amenities were observed, Press tucked a sheet around Alan's neck and backed off for a moment, pausing to appraise him. Alan saw that the man was freely perspiring.

"As you know," Sumner began, "we're going to begin a root canal for you this morning." He cleared his throat. "Under the best of circumstances, old buddy, they're painful as hell. I'm doing this as a favor to you, remember. Extractions are my bag."

"What did you mean, the 'best of circumstances?' "

Press looked away. "I meant we're going to have to pull the teeth on either side of the one we're saving." Immediately he looked back, lifting his palms in preparation for an argument. "I know what I said earlier, Alan, but I can't help it. I've studied your X-rays and those two teeth are shot."

The newspaperman's head drooped. His glance fell on the water fountain that was actually a spit-tank. Pale water swirled hungrily in its waiting depths, making it entirely clear what it was there for—and it wasn't more water. "Dammit, Press, you'll make me look the way young Brian thinks *he* looks. Like an old man with an empty face."

"Better an empty face than an empty head. Hell, Alan, a partial will make you look good as new." He smiled cheerfully, done with the argument and making his move on the patient. "Better than new!"

"But the expense!" was all Alan could get out before Nurse Crawford hove into view. She jammed a needle into his arm beneath the short-sleeved shirt, and he leaped.

Distracted by her frigid beauty, Alan was surprised to see that she held a second injecting syringe ready. Press saw his stare and, as he bent across his friend's body to force his lips apart, explained: "The pain could become pretty bad, buddy, even with the stuff we just shot into your system. Unfortunately, you can only tolerate one more shot. We want to have it ready, in case."

In case, Alan mused with desperation; *no patient likes to hear those words*. Mulling it over, he was startled when his wrists were abruptly strapped down. He peered questioningly up at the dentist, feeling hopelessly imprisoned—

—And then he was tumbling down the hills of his consciousness, plumping into the muddy morass at the bottom. He barely had the time to hear Press add, "You may get some peculiar dreams out of this, Alan, old friend. Don't believe everything you think!"

For a timeless period: nothingness. He was inert in the quicksand of his own unconscious mind: Dead for all Alan knew. Or cared. *Floating* happened; there was the slightest awareness of bodies shifting beyond his own, of things in his mouth.

Then the pain came through, jolting his awareness up a notch. Something unbelievably pointed, razor sharp, tore into his lower jaw like the full length of a sword. That was the time the sounds reached him—sounds of some madman drilling into concrete. Dimly, as he realized the drill was boring into his own yielding flesh, he was aware he was screaming. Momentarily he was ashamed; then it seemed like an excellent idea to scream some more, to get *somebody's* attention. someone who would make the dentist stop bisecting his face and skull into two segments.

Alan's betraying consciousness rose another peg, informing him not only of how piercingly he shrieked, but of how terrible, how excruciating, the pain had actually become. Buchenwald and Dacchau came to mind. There was a *grinding, wrenching* noise quite close to the eardrums—a gruesome *splintering*, as though solid bone was breaking away from the jawline, very loudly, like a mountain tumbling. He felt, just then, as the roots of his teeth were twisted and forced, like a man on a rocky ledge, holding on for dear life as the summit crumbled. And still, the tearing went on.

Finally Alan tried to thrash his arms, to awaken; but the drug and the straps on his wrists held him. That *washing* and *flushing* sensation—his dim awareness told him that was blood draining, oozing away—his own life's blood. The acute agony was simply too much to bear, and so he only screamed again, probably Ginny's name on his lips, certain that the pressure deep in his tortured mouth was popping each eyeball from its aching socket—

—When he sensed that somebody had been speaking to him; was just finishing. Someone with a voice that wasn't Press Sumner's. Yet a familiar voice, one he should undoubtedly have been able to recognize but couldn't—couldn't, because, Alan understood, he'd been told not to know that voice, and told not to remember, consciously, the orders he had just been given. Yes, there was some sort of command; he'd been told to do something. And he'd have to do it, whatever it was; he didn't know, he—

"That wasn't so bad, now, was it?"

Alan blinked, four, five times. The hinges of his jaws ached unconscionably from the rubber wedges that had been used to keep his mouth open. He stared around the surgery, seeing no one but smiling, good-buddy Press Sumner and the gorgeous iceberg who stood frigidly at the short dentist's side. His gaze swept her for signs of his own blood but he didn't see a drop.

Imagination, Alan thought; *all that was just the Old Hamhock Writer having fantasies. . . .*

After-pain struck him, then, and the customary smell of the dental office seemed accentuated and acrid. When he tried to cry out, he discovered that his entire mouth seemed swollen almost to twice its size and felt stuffed with about half-a-dozen boxes of Johnson & Johnson gauze pads. There was a terrible bloody taste in his mouth. Alan began struggling to his feet. He could live with the swelling, he supposed, but he wasn't sure he could live with that horrible *pain*. It made his eyes squint; his cheeks were so taut that they pulled at his ears. He had a headache that seemed weirdly connected to a new sore throat, and the roots of his hair throbbed.

"I want you back in here on Saturday, old buddy," Doc Sumner remarked sunnily.

The Dentist

Stunning moment. Yet when Alan stared in disbelief at the strong, small figure he found himself wondering what it was about Press that made his personality, if not his dental techniques, all at once easier to take. For the first time, Press Sumner appeared a trifle likeable to Alan—not enough to select as one's lifelong companion, but inexplicably more pleasant to be near.

If it wasn't in his damned torture chamber! Regaining his balance, Alan nodded, then hurried toward the door.

Outside, he found Luke on his feet, the boy's eyes immense with anxiety.

"Are you all right, dad?" he cried. "You screamed worse'n Brian! I never heard anything so awful!"

"I warned you," fourteen-year-old Brian muttered, still tenderly holding his cheek.

Alan stared toward them, trying to smile around his new cotton mouth. Something cool and sticky oozed from the corners. "Fine," he got out. "I'm fine."

"You're next, young man," Nurse Crawford called from behind him.

For a moment the boy froze, gaping at both the glacial beauty and his father with horror. Then, without another word, Luke turned, ran to the street door, and yanked it open. The door slammed behind him, speaking volumes.

Press appeared behind the nurse. "Where's your son?" he asked.

"Gone," Alan mumbled. Why did dentists never seem to realize one couldn't speak easily with a mouth full of blood, cotton, and pain? "Ran. Sorry."

Steadily, thoughtfully, the oral surgeon smiled. "I thought

he might. But with prior knowledge, one can always make . . . adjustments."

Alan had no idea what his friend meant but nodded, feeling too awful to care. He didn't have to worry about Luke. In a town as small as Stavenson, the child was in no danger on the streets. He went to the desk, where the immaculate nurse conceived his bill and verified the next date.

The only consolation for all the agony he'd experienced was when Nurse Crawford bent to fill out his card. There was nothing wrong with the firm young flesh he saw pressing against her bodice, but it delighted him to observe that she was wearing a heavily padded bra.

At the end of the day, Press Sumner sat in his private room, behind the surgery, lighting one of his reeking cigars. After a pause, he put his feet up on the table. The right shoe was stained with dried blood.

Too bad, he thought, that young Brian had had nothing to say about the future. The ancient Egyptians taught that children possessed special abilities for divination and prophecy. Well, that was all right. Everything else was going off on schedule.

The dentist rose and took his cigar over to the mirror on the wall. Always before, Doctor Preston Sumner had looked older than his age. His thinning hair had been a curse, except for the way it tended to build confidence in his older patients, and the rather leathery look of his skin had been part of the put-off inherent to his personality.

But now he looked into the mirror and smiled happily to himself.

The Dentist

Already the thick flesh was softening, the lines fading away. He might be wrong, it could be wishful thinking, but the hair thatching the center of his skull like flimsy railroad ties looked more luxuriant. Honest to God—or perhaps he should say, Honest to Ra, Press mused with another smile—he looked younger.

He looked . . . like it was working. Like he was becoming a modern nome god, the title given to the local deity of each ancient province of Egypt. Only the high priest or pharaoh had more influence than the nome god, in his own territory.

But that was only the first step, after all. And these were only the first signs.

In the reception area, the phone rang. Press hurried down the corridor to take the call. "Sumner here," he said into the mouthpiece.

"Press, it's Ginny. Hi."

His heartbeat accelerated. " 'Lo, Gin," he muttered. "I hope Alan is feeling better."

"Oh, he wanted me to apologize for him," she said in his ear. "He knows, now, it wasn't your fault that the pain was so intense. Really, we'd like a little company over the weekend. We'd love to have you come over for drinks and some good conversation, maybe Saturday night."

Preston Sumner saw that his cigar had gone out and didn't care. He was so happy to be asked, without Cort or someone else as the genuinely wanted guest, that he couldn't answer for a moment.

"I know it's last-minute, Press," Ginny Simmons was prattling on, "but evenings in the complex aren't the same without you."

He took a deep breath to keep his voice from trembling. "I'd love to come," he told her. "Thanks so much."

Press hung up. Everything he'd been told to expect seemed to be within reach. It was actually starting to come true!

Grinning from ear to ear, his belly ajog of its own, the dentist returned to his back room and stood for a long while, beaming at his faintly altered reflection in the mirror. *This*, he thought gaily to himself, *is worth anything*. He touched the new hair at the center of his scalp, musing. *Or even—anyone*.

SIX

"Are you sure you're all right?" Ginny inquired as she was setting the table for Wednesday night's meal. She stopped to stare at her husband, her hands full of silverware. "You look positively ashen."

Alan scarcely turned his head to peer at her, and then he didn't reply for another moment. He was sitting alone in the front room of the apartment, deep in his favorite easy chair. His legs and feet were stretched across a hassock and he had been gaping at a print on the wall by the door without seeing it.

What had made Ginny wonder was, in part, Adam's failure to read the newspaper. They subscribed to the Indianapolis *News*, in addition to Alan's own suburban paper, which simply wasn't large enough to provide information about world and national affairs. Customarily, Alan read the *News* from front to back before eating dinner. He usually discussed what he'd read with his family because it was one of the few times he felt as knowledgeable as his son Luke.

But tonight, after unfolding the newspaper, he'd simply let it slip to the floor at his feet and switched off the lamp behind his chair. Outside, yesterday's summer storm had returned, and heat lightning flashed past the apartment window, giving his face eerie hollows and a staring look. Ginny had expected Alan to feel miserable after his trip to the dentist, but he really appeared to be getting worse by the minute.

More than that, she'd decided, he didn't really seem to be hurting as much as he seemed vague and detached. Not with it. Luke had spoken to him earlier, welcoming his daddy home, and Alan had barely replied.

"I'm okay," he muttered now, sharp vertical creases showing between his brows. "I suppose it's merely the pain killer, but I feel sort of . . . peculiar. I feel as if—" He paused, blinking, staring across the distance from the front room to Ginny with an oddly baffled expression illuminated by the recurrent lightning. He seemed to be determining how much to tell her. "Nothing," he said finally, sighing.

"No, honey, I want to know," Ginny urged him. She came into the front room and sat on the edge of his chair, brushing his hair back from his forehead. "You feel as if *what?*"

"I don't know if I'm supposed to tell you."

Her mouth opened. "What does that mean?" She demanded.

THE DENTIST

"I haven't the faintest idea," he replied, looking up at her with haunted eyes. "It just seemed the right thing to say."

"Alan," she began again, firmly. "What else is bothering you besides the lousy taste in your mouth?"

He looked away, and she noticed that his left hand was trembling. "I feel as if I'm *waiting*. Waiting for something to happen. But I don't know what."

Ginny laughed, without conviction. "Drugs do funny things to people," she observed. She rose, bustingly. "C'mon. Call Luke to dinner for me, okay?"

"Sure," he answered her with more willingness than he felt, making himself rise, and starting down the short carpeted corridor toward the boy's room, steadying himself with an outflung hand against the beige wall. When he moved this way, all the afternoon pain came charging back in full force. But oddly enough, he realized, it was very nearly a relief. The pain neatly distracted his attention from the pressures, confusion, and sensations of waiting which lurked in his mind. Agony was, at least, relatively understandable. Rocking slightly, he squinted into Luke's open bedroom. "Luke, my main man," he called, "it's time to eat."

The nine-year-old lay atop the bedspread, a rust-colored covering ornamented with cartoon characters. They'd bought the bedspread, back when they thought Luke would be more intrigued by Donald Duck and Superman than the ancient Etruscans. "I'm not really hungry, dad," Luke responded feebly.

"Sure, you are," Alan argued. He mustered all the good humor he could. "I don't know where all that grub you eat goes, since you're as skinny as a rail. But I've apprehended my man. And he's always hungry."

"Wow, not tonight." The boy's bespectacled gaze met Alan's and there were tears behind the heavy lenses. "I guess I shouldn't have run from Uncle Press and you today. Boy, my teeth hurt like the dickens." He tried a wan smile. "It's because I'm way too old to have baby teeth anymore."

Alan froze, a hand on either side of the doorframe. Dizzy. He was unable to move an inch; time was suspended. *Teeth, my teeth*; the word thundered inside his head. *Teeth*. It echoed through his mind in swiftly-spiraling circles of sound: *teeth; teeth; teeth; teeth*—and behind the word, like some clever ventriloquist stooped behind a leering dummy, there were . . . *other* words, as well. Words heard only by Alan Simmons' subconscious mind, as it captured control.

Alan nodded, slowly, understanding. Then he blinked and returned to the moment. Somewhere in the cosmos his personal clock began ticking again. "Those baby teeth of yours," he said. "They have to come out." It was flat; delivered in a metallic monotone. His head bobbed in agreement with himself. *"Tonight."*

The boy sat up, frightened. "How, dad? You gonna take me t'see Uncle Press at night?"

"Oh, no." Alan shook his head. *"I'm* going to pull 'em." Just saying that caused him to feel better. Strangely, it was liberating to seem to have made the decision, to be all firm and fatherly about it. "The way little kids' teeth have been pulled out for hundreds of years." He paused. "With a string."

Luke had drawn near to him now and looked up with an expression of utter consternation. "You mean," he began, swallowing hard, "with the string tied to my bad teeth and a—a *doorknob?* Like in comics?"

THE DENTIST

Alan nodded. "Right after dinner. We are not going to mess around any longer with a minor little problem of this kind." He turned to head for the dining room. "Wash your hands and let's get going, old buddy."

He was halfway down the corridor when he wondered why he'd called Luke "old buddy." He never had before.

When Luke came to the table, white-faced and anxious, he slid into his appointed chair. In tribute to Alan's pain from the extractions and root canal, Ginny had settled for her famous vegetable soup.

"Dad's gonna pull my teeth himself," Luke reported, half-hoping for his mother to intervene. "With a string."

She turned instantly to Alan, concerned. "That's a pretty old-fashioned way to do things these days," she said, ladling soup into three bowls. "Isn't it?"

"Well, I could use a hammer," he said, hiding a smile.

"Dad!" Luke exclaimed, blanching.

"See?" he said blithely. "Things could always get worse."

"Couldn't you wait until Saturday?" Ginny tried. "You have to go back, and I go for my own examination Saturday. Surely we could squeeze Luke in."

"My mom always told me the old ways were best," he replied, sipping soup. The storm outside had lowered the temperature. Ginny had come up with exactly the right meal. Now she was fixing peanut butter sandwiches for Alan and Luke, to supplement the soup, but watching him intently. "And I think she's right."

"What a justification," Ginny burst out, plopping Alan's sandwich on a plate and shoving it to him in pique. "Your mother was always as modern as day-after-tomorrow. The only thing old-fashioned she had in your house was your father."

Alan did not answer. He finished his soup and sandwich quickly.

"Are you done?" Alan asked Luke moments later.

"Honey, he's barely had half his soup," Ginny protested.

But the nine-year-old nodded and stood, shakily. "Let's get it over with," he said very bravely.

Alan clapped his shoulder and went out to the small tool container beneath the kitchen sink, rummaging around. "Aha!" he cried, pushing aside a lug wrench and six or seven loose penny nails. He held up a ball of white twine. "This stuff is good and strong. It won't break on us."

Luke wiped his steaming glasses on his shirt-tail.

Ginny had followed them. Standing above Alan, she touched his shoulder lightly. "Do you really have to go through with this?"

"Certainly," he said brightly. "Why don't you stop frightening the boy?"

"Honey, *why?*" she demanded. "If you don't do it properly, you could hurt Luke badly."

He paused a moment, halted by his affection for them both. Pain squeezed back into his head, but it was the pain of resistance to command. He tried to consider his motivations. "I suppose I just want to spare Luke the kind of thing Press put me through." He listened to his words and knew they were, at least, honest ones. "I really believe he'd hurt Luke more than I ever could."

Ginny bit her lip. "Very well. You should know what you're doing."

Yes, I should, Alan thought as he took Luke by the hand

The Dentist

and led him back down the hallway to his and Ginny's bedroom. *But I wonder if I do.*

He secured the twine to Luke's lower milk-tooth and continued to work moistly in his mouth. "I'm going to try an experiment in the hope of making this easier for you," he explained to the boy. "I was a Boy Scout once, and I knew about string. I'm trying to rig it so that I can yank all three teeth out at the same time."

Ginny watched with her arms crossed, paled. "So he'll only have to go through it once," she said, nodding. "I hope it works."

"There!" Alan exclaimed, standing back to evaluate his handiwork. Three strands were knotted in such a way that they were linked to the central long strand. He gave a little experimental jerk to make sure the tension on the strands was equal, and Luke reflexively said a mild "Ow." Alan slowly nodded. "It should work."

He turned without another word and tied the long central strand to the doorknob of his and Ginny's bedroom, allowing just a little slack. "Tell you what, old buddy," he called over his shoulder. "We'll put those teeth of yours under your pillow, when they're out, and I'll just bet the Tooth Fairy will come and leave you some money for them. Maybe a quarter for each tooth."

Luke's eyes narrowed suspiciously behind his glasses. "Is the Tooth Fairy anything like Santa Claus?" he asked warily.

"Well, he's a generous old guy, too," Alan replied with a laugh. "What he *does* with those teeth, I don't really know."

"Cort was telling me some myths about teeth," Ginny put in, as Alan returned to Luke and began positioning him. "For one thing, it's good that we're doing this before midnight.

It used to be believed that pulling teeth brought evil spirits, if it was done after twelve o'clock."

Alan glanced over at her with a grin. "Frankly, for me to believe in superstitions like that is, well—just like pulling teeth!"

"Ouch!" Ginny said, managing a laugh. She turned her back, incapable of watching what would happen next. "And Cort said that dreaming of teeth falling out meant someone was bound to die."

"Gee, honey, that story is sure to help old Luke," Alan remarked. He had Luke the way he wanted him now and his own hand was on the bedroom door, ready. *Why am I doing this?* he wondered. *Where did I get a crazy notion like this?*

Ginny glanced over her shoulder and saw that little Luke was fascinated by the old tales. Even with the string leading tautly from his mouth, his curiosity was aroused. She tried to remember more of what Cort Devalyn had said that night. "Then too, it's still believed in some parts of the world that you can prevent all kinds of problems, including toothache, by wearing a little bag around your neck containing the forelegs and one hindleg of a mole. Or, even better—"

The door slammed and Luke screamed wrenchingly.

"—Teeth from a corpse," Ginny blurted, turning to embrace Luke. Blood was gushing from his mouth, and she knew it was getting on her clothes but she didn't care. She glanced up at Alan. He was staring admiringly at the trio of baby teeth—the startling teeth of Luke's birth—innocent and bloody in his cupped palm. She snarled at him: "Bastard."

Then, to her surprise, Alan slowly sank to his knees and pitched forward on his face.

* * *

THE DENTIST

Both her men were in bed at last, Luke wearily tucked into his own, while Alan reclined on theirs, looking guilty as sin.

"Why in the world did you insist on that?" she asked him, holding a damp cold cloth on his forehead. It was the third she'd brought Alan in the last forty minutes. She didn't know whether she hated him for causing Luke pain or loved him because he was merely an old, feeble, silly macho-style husband—and because he'd succeeded. Luke's teeth were cleanly pulled, and there was plenty of room for the permanent ones to come in.

Alan gestured helplessly. "Gee, darlin', I honestly don't know." He looked sheepish. His mouth was still swollen; it gave him the look of a prizefighter who'd lost on a technical knockout in the first round. He managed a rueful smile. "Like the saying goes, it sounded like a good idea at the time."

"Well, damn you, it wasn't!" Ginny snapped, taking the washcloth away and sitting on the edge of the bed. She had removed her blood-spotted dress and wore only a bra and panties. "He should have gone with me on Saturday. A competent professional is going to handle my dental work, and—"

"Nonsense, my dear, *I'll* take care of it!"

At the maniacal sound of his voice, she turned to him. Leering at her like a cutrate vampire, Alan was on his knees in the center of the bed, eyes bugging out, fingers clawed, his tongue popping in and out like a lizard's.

Before she knew it, he had thrown her flat on her back beside him and was laughing, poking his fingers beneath her bra. The surprise was so great, and she loved him so much, that she felt her nipples growing erect beneath his touch.

93

"Idiot," she growled. "I'm the only woman in town with a thirty-year-old teenager."

"And I shall demonstrate my youth and vitality to you by the swiftest possible means," he cried with a smile, slipping her panties down and kissing her in the soft spot below her navel.

Ginny remembered to ask one thing before she gave herself to their pleasure fully. "What'd you do with Luke's teeth?"

"Where they belong, me proud beauty," Alan replied, changing character but not leers. "Right under his pillow." He knelt on the bed and drew her head toward him. "But I've always wondered how wise it is to encourage fairies to visit our son in the middle of the night."

"You're ridiculous," Ginny whispered, smiling. "You're really weird."

"It's the nature of the literary brute," he answered. And then he said no more.

When the thunderclap crashed, seemingly yards above the house, Luke opened his eyes sleepily to stare into the darkness of his bedroom.

He had never been quick to believe that the dark concealed all manner of terrifying monsters. Oh, it was true that he wasn't too sure about the closet if the door was ajar. Once, Luke was positive, he'd seen pale, skeletal things hulking just inside. *Waiting.* Even though he had had to go to the bathroom, he'd stayed right where he was, absolutely immobile. And the morning afterward, he had found the coathangers in the closet swinging gently, making the clicking sound he'd heard in the night, and had told himself what an icky little jerk he was.

THE DENTIST

Now, however, as he looked across the lonely endless acres of bedroom, Luke's heart nearly stopped in his chest. He had been right, after all!

Because one of THEM was free of the closet. Luke saw its tall, black shape right now, groping and slithering across the room—directly toward him.

"Our Father," Luke prayed silently, shutting his eyes so tight the places where his milk teeth had been ached painfully, "which art in Heaven . . ."

Footsteps, creaking on the floorboards. Something with weight, something awful, crept close. And closer.

He lost his place in the prayer. He began again, vaulted to the important part: "And lead us not into temptation but *deliver* us from *evil* . . ." *Near,* the damned thing was, *near now*! He could hear its hot dragon-breath with his eyes closed, *sense* the monster with every cell and every pore of his body. "Deliver us from *evil*," he mouthed it, his lips moving; "*deliver* us; *deliver* us!"

Unable to keep his eyes shut, Luke opened them, staring—

And saw a man's deep chest before him, arms reaching—*reaching toward him!*

Luke bit his upper lip till he tasted blood, squelching the scream that welled-up, saw and felt the man's hands lift both his head and his pillow away from the bed! *He's taking me with him!* the boy shrieked silently.

Instead, the arms lowered Luke, and the pillow, back in place and the figure turned. Already it was at the door, opening it into the dark hallway. Lightning flickered softly at the window. Luke had just the time to see one white, hairy arm and hand . . .

And then it was gone.

Luke inhaled. He realized he'd scarcely breathed while the monster was in his room. *One, two, three,* he counted, staring at the gaping doorway. *Four, five, six* . . .

When he'd counted to sixty, a full minute, Luke sat up in bed, sweaty, and turned on the lamp on his nightstand. He lifted the pillow, and stared with astonishment.

Dad had promised the Tooth Fairy would leave a quarter for each tooth. Seventy-five cents.

Whatever it had been—Fairy or monster—had left him something much better; a crisp, new, ten-dollar bill.

SEVEN

"You know you want to," he told her, trying again to undress her.

Nurse Ethel Crawford was locked in a sort of improvised wrestler's hold in the arms of Doctor Preston Sumner, more or less willingly; but she was slow to thaw. She'd gone out with him this Wednesday night because he was her boss and because, to her surprise, he'd suddenly seemed to flash a measure of unexpected charm. But several heated kisses after drinks at the Roustabout Bar seemed more than adequate payment for the minimal good time the dentist had provided, and, in the automobile's darkness, Doc Sumner's newfound charms had faded fully away.

J. N. Williamson

"People who always do what they want end up in trouble," she told him, trying to reassert her icy daytime control. "After all, Doctor, this is only our first date. There'll be other times."

"That's what college girls always tell you," Press argued, his tone a mild whine. He'd found himself quite incapable of keeping his hands to himself. They appeared to have a life of their own tonight. Perhaps it was because beautiful Ethel was the first girl he'd pursued since Angela left, or perhaps it was other, darker things entirely. He couldn't tell. "They also say how much they want to get to know you first, so you'll respect them. But we work together every day, Ethel. We already know each other, and I already respect you."

"Is that a threat?" she inquired, frowning. "Are you telling me that if I don't come across, you're going to fire me?"

Press released her at once and faced the front of the car. They were parked behind a liquor store in Stevenson's one good-sized shopping center and it was both very dark and isolated outside. His fingers drummed the steering wheel of his four-year-old Chrysler as he frowned. "I'm not the kind of man to blackmail women, Nurse Crawford. I want you to make love to me because you—" His voice drifted away as he remembered certain key facts. He felt his breath catch in his chest.

"Because I find you attractive?" she finished for him, touching his hand. Obviously, Ethel Crawford thought, this farce was over. Now she had to restore his ego or, regardless of what he'd said, face the possibility of being fired. There weren't that many good jobs in Stevenson. "I *do*, of course, Press. It's just that you're still married. Your wife might come back. And—"

THE DENTIST

Doctor Sumner turned on the interior lights. He turned his head to face her, and smiled as gently and winningly as he could.

Nurse Crawford looked at his face, and into his eyes, and her own breath caught. "What was I saying?" she asked.

"Does it matter?" he asked softly, engagingly. "Haven't we used enough words now?"

Impossible, she thought wonderingly, *but the dentist seems so different. Now there is such kindness and compassion in those eyes, such wisdom! And that cute, silly little bald spot— his smile—he's not physically threatening the way tall, powerful men are . . .*

"Take your clothes off, dear," Press told her pleasantly.

She paused, but then she obeyed. Her blouse, her bra, her skirt and underpants followed one another to the back seat. When she wore nothing but stockings, shoes and a smile, the dentist crooked his finger and mouthed the words: "Come here."

She did, joyfully pressing herself against him from the waist up, her fingers running down his anatomy, caressing him.

Excited, the dentist kissed her on the mouth quite hard. When he drew back, blood framed one of her front teeth like a picture. He looked at it, licking his lips, more aroused than he could ever recall. "You have exceptionally fine teeth, Nurse Crawford," he said in a nearly professional tone. "Perfect molars and incisors. Shall we get into the backseat now?" He turned off the interior light. "You'll find it more comfortable there."

Ethel nodded, licked away the small seepage of blood, and opened the passenger door. When he saw her pale buttocks

99

dipping through the back door, Press began unzipping his pants.

But to his utter astonishment, by the time he was ducking his own head through the back door, Nurse Crawford was again dressing. He put out a hand. She shuddered, flinching away from him.

"Whatever is the matter?" he asked, one foot in the backseat.

"Don't get in here!" she ordered him, fastening her lacy bra. Already she was clothed from the waist down. Quite simply, the spell had been broken when she looked away from the dentist. To her relief as well as her mortification, Nurse Crawford had regained control of her own desires and wishes. "Just drive me home, *Doctor* Sumner. *This minute!*"

He paused, trying hard to get her to look at his face. "You know you want to," he said a second time.

"Oh no, I do *not!*" she exclaimed, fastening her blouse and then staring out the window. "You are sadly mistaken."

Press Sumner paused, considering. He took a deep breath. "Very well." He got behind the steering wheel again, thinking furiously. *Maybe it requires the next step in the plan. Maybe it requires development of the* entire *plan, with everything that means. But sooner or later, Nurse Crawford,* the dentist thought, turning the key in the ignition, *you'll want to. You, and any other woman I want.*

In the rearview mirror he saw her daubing the blood away from her injured front tooth.

On Thursday morning, Ginny Simmons decided it was time to do something about Press Sumner's wife. To her, it seemed perfectly obvious that the nice fellow desperately

THE DENTIST

missed lovely, redhaired Angela and certainly their sweet little girl, Lucy. What was a friend for, if not pitching in to help when the going became really rough?

To have company on the visit to Angela's apartment, Ginny telephoned Ellie Devalyn and asked her to come along. It was true that Angela had wanted no one but Ginny to know her whereabouts, and ordinarily Ginny kept a confidence better than anyone she knew. But if Angela got mad at them, she'd simply have to get angry. Together, the two of them—Ginny and jolly, likeable Ellie—could surely persuade the pretty redhead to return home. Clearly, that was in her own best interest.

Steady, reliable husbands like Press Sumner weren't exactly a dime a dozen!

Once they parked, it took Ginny and Ellie only minutes to find Angela's apartment number.

The front door was unlocked. It moved easily inward when they touched the knob.

"It smells stale in here," Ellie said from behind her friend, immediately uneasy.

"I wonder why she left the door unlocked." Ginny was moving slowly ahead into the front room. "Angela?" she called. "Angela, are you home?"

"I don't like this," the overweight blonde murmured, uneasily following Ginny well into the room. "I haven't said a word about it, but Angela has been under terribly planetary influences for absolutely *ages* now."

Ginny put her purse down on the coffee table and glanced at Ellie with a faint frown. "Why are we whispering this way?" she demanded. "We're behaving as if we'd walked into a mortuary or something."

Ellie's eyes grew enormous. "You don't suppose she could be back in the bedroom," she said carefully, *"not alone?"*

"Now you're being ridiculous," Ginny snapped, wheeling and heading down the short corridor to the bedrooms. "Until some little thing happened to them—some crazy little problem that they'll work out and laugh about someday—Angela and Press were practically a perfect couple."

Ellie trailed after her friend, startled. Angela was a nice enough person, but since when did anybody apply the adjective "perfect" to that horrid little dentist? She had seen him a few days ago; she scarcely believed that he could have changed *that* much.

"Look at this," Ginny said, inside a room that was obviously Angela's. Her expression was one of deep concern. "All of her clothes are still here, but the bed is unmade and everything's dusty. Ellie, I don't think Angela's been here for days."

"Maybe she just went somewhere for a brief vacation?" the blonde suggested, lifting a crumpled blouse from a chair and then putting it down again.

"And left her clothes behind? And a mess like this?" Ginny gestured to the vanity table. "And all her makeup? Come on!"

"I suppose you're right." Idly, Ellie pushed open a connecting door and found the bathroom. Two towels, long since dried, hung over the edge of the tub. She ambled to the opposite door and looked inside, discovering that it was little Lucy's room.

"Ginny, come in here! Something really strange is going on!"

Ginny came running, stopping beside Ellie.

While a few items of clothing remained in Lucy's room, apparently dropped as if while packing, most of the girl's things were gone. This room had been cleaned out.

"It's . . . as if Lucy went somewhere by herself," Ginny began, her gaze sweeping from one corner of the room to the other, "while Angela stayed behind."

"Except that she isn't here either," Ellie reminded her, shivering. "What kind of sense does that make?"

"Hell, El, I really don't know." Ginny frowned. "But look over there."

Ellie heard the tremor in Ginny's voice, then stared where she pointed.

In the closet, face down, an enormous, frilly doll reclined in sharp neglect. Ginny crossed the room to it and picked it up, holding it across her arm. Memories of her own dolls, and how attached she had once been to them, flooded her mind with fresh anxiety. "This was Lucy's favorite," she whispered, turning to stare at Ellie. "She took it with her everywhere she went."

"Dear Lord," the blonde murmured, standing close to her friend and touching the doll's painted red lips. "What's going on here, Gin? Do you think we should telephone the police?"

Ginny hesitated. "No, not over a doll that's been left behind. There's nothing here that would mean a thing to the authorities—*male* authorities. They'd just tell us that the two of them left too quickly to remember everything, that Angela planned to buy all new clothes to celebrate being separated from Press." Her fingers clutched Ellie's plump arm. "I have to see Press myself Saturday morning, when Alan goes back for a checkup. I'll see what he wants to do."

"But Ginny—"

"Well, after all, he's still legally Angela's husband, and I'm sure he wouldn't want anything to happen—either to her, or to the little girl." She rested the doll in a chair and patted its artificial hair.

"You don't think Press knows anything about this?" Ellie asked grimly.

"Press? Of course not!" Ginny laughed. "I know neither of us liked him much in the past, but there's no sense in getting all paranoid about this." She started back toward the front door of the apartment. "Really, he's a very nice person once you get to know him better."

"You and Cort," the heavy blonde sighed, following the brunette. "What you see in the little creep I'll never know. Frankly, I'm inclined to call the authorities."

"Hold it." Ginny headed for something on the floor beside the front closet. Ellie saw that it was a scrap of paper. Ginny stooped to retrieve it, then looked at it. "Looks like it's come out of an encyclopedia, or something." Ginny announced. "The edge of the paper is ragged, like it had been accidentally torn from the book."

"What does it say?" Ellie asked.

Ginny cleared her throat and read it. " 'The Pyramid Texts explain that an *Akh* is the spirit of a god, and resides in heaven. When an ordinary man dies, his own *Akh* eventually goes to heaven too. Yet there are indications that this may have been an Egyptian smokescreen used to deceive their enemies. The *Book of the Dead* declares, for example, "My mouth is strong; and I am equipped against the Akhs." Apparently an Akh, said to be observable as a beam of light, was actually *demonic* in origin and in some fashion was employed to destroy enemies of the Egyptians and their gods.' " Ginny lowered the paper, looking confused. "Ellie, what a strange thing to find here in Angela Sumner's apartment! She wasn't interested in exotic topics like—like Egyptology, was she?"

Ellie wasn't looking at Ginny any longer.

She wasn't planning to phone the authorities, either. She was starting out the door of the deserted apartment, deeply upset and already lost in her own private worries. She knew only one person in Stevenson, Indiana, who was apt to be fascinated by the ancient Egyptians.

Her own husband, Cort Devalyn.

EIGHT

When Ginny Simmons told Alan about her visit to Angela's apartment, he tugged thoughtfully on his ear and then decided to speak his piece.

"This isn't like you, darling," he said slowly. It was Saturday morning, and they were due at Preston Sumner's office in an hour. He sipped his coffee another moment before continuing, then covered Ginny's hands with his own. "Look, hon, this isn't really any of our business. It's Press' and Angela's."

She tugged her hands free and glared at him. "I thought I explained how the apartment looked. But maybe I didn't make myself clear to you. Alan, it looked for all the world like Angela had—had *disappeared*, but like someone had taken their little girl."

He chuckled deeply in his throat. "You've been reading too many mystery novels," he said. He hadn't put a shirt over his T-shirt yet, and his slender arms made him look more youthful than ever. "This is little-bitty Stevenson, not New York or Detroit. The last killing on this chunk of ground was one hundred and fifty years ago when some Indian scalped a farmer in a squabble over his horse."

"I didn't say anything about killings," Ginny said in a breath, her green eyes widening. "Oh, my God, Alan, you don't suppose—"

He laughed openly this time. "Now I know your imagination is running away with you. Sweetheart, there must be a good hundred explanations for where Angela and Lucy have gone. Your own idea, that Angela went somewhere to buy new clothes, is a decent explanation. Lots of divorced women want to buy new things with their own money, to get their ex-husbands completely out of their systems."

"But what about Lucy?"

Alan shrugged and looked back at her with an easy smile. "I imagine Angela asked some friend we don't know— somebody over in Indianapolis maybe—to take care of Lucy while she's away."

"Children don't leave their favorite dolls behind!" Ginny exclaimed valiantly, glaring at him again. "I would never have gone away without mine."

"You would if your mother was leaving quickly and just grabbed you by your hand," he reminded her, getting to his feet. "Or if she picked you up while you were asleep."

Ginny looked after him, shouting, "You have an answer to

everything, don't you? You're like the Germans during World War II, who wouldn't believe anything really terrible was going on a mile away!"

He stopped and pivoted, angry. "I don't think I like being compared to people like that," he said flatly with a frown. "Look at it this way: If you bring it up to Press, he'll realize you know where Angela is staying. And he'll ask you. Are you ready to betray Angela's confidence all the way?"

Ginny looked away from his hot gaze, her lips compressed. "You're right about that," she relented, tapping her newly polished fingernails on the tabletop.

He smiled lightly and crossed quickly to her. His hands draped on her shoulders, he stooped a little to give her a quick kiss on the mouth. "Honey, I'd give you great odds that if you'll only wait a few days and then go back to her apartment, you'll find both Angela and Lucy have returned and everything is just great. But if you don't, by the time that happens Press will know where they've gone and Angela will be mad as hell at you."

Ginny sighed. "I only wanted to be sure nothing bad was happening," she said simply, turning her cheek. "I was so worried about them."

"I can understand that. Look, let's do it this way." Alan paused. "You're having the whole gang over here tonight, right? Press, Cort and Ellie, maybe Dennis and Mary Grazell? Well, I'll ask Press a few careful questions. If he knows how Angela is getting along, if he's seen their little girl lately—that kind of question, okay? I'm sure he'll tell us whatever he knows about them, and you'll have accomplished your purpose without embarrassing yourself or anyone else. What do you think?"

She nodded her agreement and told him the plan was fine. He left the room and went back to the bedroom to finish dressing.

But insistent, puzzling questions nagged at her, all the same, and she couldn't shake them even after she was in Doc Sumner's dental chair: What good would it do for Alan to ask Press about Angela and Lucy if he simply didn't know—or if, for some crazy reason, he was lying? How would that get them back?

And most important of all, if her friends needed her desperately *this very moment*, wasn't she making a terrible mistake by doing nothing?

To Ginny's pleasant surprise, her complete annual checkup that Saturday wasn't even half as bad as she'd expected, particularly after Alan's groaning complaints. While Press Sumner urged her to come back Tuesday, three days later, to fill a cavity, he not only gave her a generally clean bill of health but treated her with gentleness and consideration. In addition, he was full of quips and compliments, entirely gallant. All in all, her estimation of the dentist rose.

Alan had gone back that day primarily for an examination of the work Doc Sumner had done Wednesday and knew he'd have to return, with Ginny, on Tuesday. For more extensive work. But even though the oral surgeon only prodded here and there, his every jab seemed to bring sharp and reawakened agony.

When he remarked on it to Ginny after they left the office for their customary Saturday grocery shopping, still blinking tears out of his eyes, his wife laughed. "I don't think it's so damned funny," he barked at her, wishing that he hadn't asked her to drive. "I tell you, Press has lost his stuff. Every time he touches me there's pain."

"He's as gentle as a baby," Ginny contradicted him, turning the wheel to enter the Safeway supermarket lot on the edge of Indianapolis. She was still smarting, herself, from the way Alan had chided her about Angela's abandoned apartment, and this was as good a way to get back at him as any. "I tell you, *men!*" she exclaimed. "If it isn't *ab*-so-lutely comfortable, if they don't have *to*tal service and *in*stant relief, they can't stand it!"

Alan leaned forward in his seat, outraged. "Ask Brian Devalyn, if you don't believe me that Press is getting too rough!" he exploded. "*He* was there on Wednesday! Brian will tell you!"

Ginny giggled and pulled into a parking slot, cutting the engine. She opened the door and got out. Then her pretty, teasing face looked in at him, smirking. "*Fourteen-year-old* Brian Devalyn! Whom, if I haven't lost my powers of recognition, is also All-American hotshot *male* Brian Devalyn—man-to-*be!*"

Laughing, she closed the door sweetly and wriggled three fingers at him.

He stayed where he was, swearing colorfully to himself between clenched jaws. Couples drifted through the shopping center. Alan avoided looking at them. When a nice old lady happened to glance his way, he glowered fiercely at her. Vowing not to mention how much he hurt, even if he was dying, he went in to the Safeway after Ginny.

That night, lanky Cort and chubby Ellie arrived first, smiling and hugging the Simmonses, followed by Mary and

Dennis Grazell, whom Ginny and Alan had half-adopted. Each Simmons had been there when the younger couple had become embroiled in their first fight, speaking encouragingly but separately to them. Another couple who had moved in recently, Max and Betty Werlin, came next.

Last to arrive were Press Sumner and his date. To the newspaperman's surprise, the lovely woman on the dentist's arm was the gorgeous, chilly nurse, Ethel Crawford. The one whom Alan believed Press had discovered riding on an ice floe. Press was patting his lips with a handkerchief when he opened the door. To Alan's amazement, he caught a smear of blurred lipstick before it vanished into the dentist's suit pocket.

More than that, Alan mused as the two moved into the apartment, unless his Old Newsbeagle Eye was warped, sexy Ethel was higher than a kite. Or at any rate, he amended his thoughts as he followed after them, she was certainly not herself. The girl's face seemed slack, disoriented.

It occurred to Alan, as he got them a beer, that it would be hard to keep his promise to Ginny. How could he grill Press about his wife with Nurse Crawford nearby?

The first few hours of the Saturday get-together were spent talking and listening to a rich variety of the Simmons records, ranging from the latest rock and John Denver, Ginny's favorite, to Peggy Lee and the old Dorsey albums. An occasional flare seemed to rise on the wings of laughter as someone told an offcolor joke.

But as the evening wore on, Alan found himself drinking more than usual. His gums still throbbed, he felt a little mad at the dentist, and with four imported beers under his belt—believing that he was as penetrative as Mike Wallace—Alan

The Dentist

asked a question loudly enough that the other guests stopped to listen: "Tell me, Press," he began firmly, "when did they begin replacing teeth with other things? Like gold?"

The oral surgeon had been talking persuasively to Ethel, and looked up with an expression of mild annoyance. "Well, we've found gold teeth in mummies. But that was probably ornamental or religious, and may have been done after their death." He looked up at his best friend, who was nearby. "You'll have to ask Cort for more exact information."

Alan licked the corner of his mouth and turned to the lanky anthropology teacher. "Tell us all about dentistry, Cortland."

Cort smiled down. He was standing behind his wife Ellie's chair, his glasses fogged, his eyes only partly visible. "That's a tall order," he stated.

"Well, you're a tall teacher," Alan replied, not unreasonably. "A tall order for a tall teacher to talk about a tall history. Eminently suitable, I'd say."

"Okay," Cort said lightly, holding his can of Miller's against one temple. "Well, actually *replacing* teeth probably didn't begin until a few hundred years before Christ when Herodotus spoke of dentistry becoming a specialized subject. Then Hippocrates discussed the number of teeth in someone's mouth in relation to longevity."

"They made toothpicks of quill or wood in the first century," little Luke piped up.

"Where did you come from?" Alan asked goodhumoredly, rumpling his son's hair.

"Do you really want me to explain *that* in front of all these people?" the boy demanded with an impish grin. The remark got a huge laugh from everybody.

"You have a truly exceptional boy, old friend," Press Sumner said, his small eyes appraising Luke. "While I bow to my dear friend Cort in his knowledge of dental history—among countless other things—I do know a good deal about the superstitions involving teeth. Would you like to hear some of them, Luke?"

Ginny put her glass down. She was sitting with Mary and Dennis Grazell and looked alarmed. "Are you sure that's wise, Press?"

Alan chuckled. "You were telling the kid some of the wild stories Cort told you," he reminded her. "What's the difference?"

Ginny's glance passed from her husband's face, to Press', to Cort's and back to Press. She colored. "None, I suppose."

"Tell me," Luke encouraged him, all eyes.

Press' gaze rose briefly, flickered toward Cort's own eyes and drifted down again. "Well, Luke, in some parts of the world people believe that if you take a boy's tooth and place it near a rat-hole, then his teeth will be as razor-sharp and pointed as the rat's. In many sections of Europe, and even in areas of these United States, teeth are taken and mutilated, then worn as a talisman."

Cort had moved to stand behind Press. Now his hand dropped heavily to the dentist's shoulder. "I'm inclined to agree with Ginny," he said. Alan saw that he was beginning to perspire. "Those stories may be a trifle lurid for a lad Luke's age."

"I only had one more," Press persisted. For the first time Alan realized that Press was quietly, unobtrusively drunk. "In ancient Greece, Luke, they believed that widely-spaced teeth allowed the inflow of a soul and of someone's vital energies. It was a sneaky way of getting power from the other person."

"Which is logical enough, in its silly way," Cort said quickly, seizing the spotlight, "since the lips are the first external organs taking shape in the foetus."

"Tell us about the ancient Egyptians."

It was Ellie who spoke. Cort thought her voice sounded somewhat strident and forced. He didn't budge. He continued looking at Luke Simmons, expressionlessly, aware that the boy was watching his every move.

"Well, like many other people of yore," the anthropologist said at last, his tone entirely level and relaxed, "the Egyptians believed in many peculiar things. Fantastic things, actually. Signs of all kinds. Amulets, to protect them against evil. A series of special rites intended to bring one good health. That sort of bizarre thing."

"They believed in the Akh too," Ellie spoke up again, her voice too loud. "Didn't they, Cort?"

Now he felt both Ginny and Alan Simmons' eyes upon him, strongly, and Cort cleared his throat. What was Ellie driving at? "Not necessarily. It depends entirely upon the particular period of Egyptian history and—and the particular location. Besides, an Akh was thought to mean a variety of things."

"It still seems odd to me," Alan began, sounding more sober now, "that you know so much about dentistry. I would have thought that was Press' area of expertise."

Cort's look at Alan was cold, flat. "The truth is, Alan, Press and I have learned that we have more in common than meets the eye. Many . . . *shared* interests."

"It's my everlasting good fortune," Press injected with

warmth, "that I've made a friend of Cort. And joined this group of his friends, of course." He cleared his throat, looked directly into Ethel Crawford's eyes for a moment, then loosened his collar. "I've never been a guy whom people automatically liked, the way they do Cort. Can you understand—*any* of you?—what it means to be lonely? What it means to be by yourself?"

For a moment nobody answered. Then Ginny did. "You had Angela," she said. She, too, avoided his gaze. One look at his serious, apparently tender eyes would have prevented her from doing what she felt she must. "And nobody mentions her any more, Press. It's almost as if she—died."

Now the dentist looked straight at Ginny and his lower lip trembled. "A week or so ago," he began, "one of my patients saw Angela at another apartment complex here in Stevenson. Lucy was with her, of course. They were returning after shopping at that big Hook Drugs—do you know the one I mean?"

Surprised, Ginny nodded. She knew it, all right. It was only a block from Angela's deserted apartment.

"I could have gone there, easily located Angela's new apartment," Press went on, his head high, "but I didn't. It was enough to know they were all right. Especially when my patient told me that she spoke to Angie on my behalf, told her how much I wanted to visit little Lucy." He swallowed, hard. "It seems she has a restraining order against me and means to wait until the divorce to allow me to see Lucy again. Under those circumstances, Ginny, can you understand why I don't talk about them?"

Alan and Ginny exchanged glances. He was wondering how Press' remark could be validated without insulting him.

116

The Dentist

Then Mary Grazell spoke. The youngest member of the group, barely twenty-one, she was an exceptionally pretty brownette with wide eyes and a sensual mouth. "I'm the patient Doctor Sumner is talking about," she said softly, feeling that she might be intruding. "I knew how very lonely he was for the little girl—either Dennis or I would be bound to feel that way, too, if either of us couldn't see our baby, Alaina—and tried to help by speaking with Mrs. Sumner. I really don't know w-why she was so stubborn about it, but she . . . didn't want to let the doctor know where she and the little girl were. Under any circumstances." Abruptly, she shrugged her sweatered shoulders, looking young and fresh. "I just did what I could."

Dennis, her husband, grinned at the others. He was a likeable young man no more than an inch taller than the dentist. He wore a neatly trimmed mustache intended to make him seem older. "Mary's way of trying to please both Doctor and Mrs. Sumner was by tellin' the doc the name of Angela's complex and urging her to telephone the doc."

Preston Sumner swallowed. He took a step forward in order to be seen by everybody. "I'll never be able to tell you what it has meant to me to find such fine, new friends at such a trying point in my life." He looked down briefly at Ethel Crawford and squeezed her shoulder. Then he touched every face in the Simmons apartment with his sensitive eyes. "Your support means everything to me!"

Alan stepped forward at once, an embarrassed little smile on his face, putting out a hand. "I think maybe we were a little put off by your profession at first, Press, but we're all glad you're here with us now." He squeezed the dentist's hand hard, in sincere camaraderie. "You're really a helluva guy."

"I told you he was something special," Cort remarked with a grin.

Ellie looked at Ginny, who looked back; and a message was exchanged. Each of them responded to Press' newfound charm and his obvious need for friendship, but neither of them could forget Angela's deserted apartment—and, also unspoken but clear: neither of them knew what to do about it.

It was perfectly obvious to chunky, blonde Ellie that Press, with a momentary alcoholic buzz, had begun to say things that her husband Cort didn't think he should say. Things about teeth, talismans, and mutilation among the ancients. But where that antique mumbo-jumbo might have been leading, Ellie couldn't imagine. It surely made no sense. But Ginny was correct, Ellie felt, in identifying certain exceptional changes in the little dentist. He *was* nicer. She could feel it herself. She discovered it was impossible to dislike him the way she had before.

But what had Press done to become so much more acceptable, even sexy, all at once? *Was* Cort helping him in some way? And, if so, why—what could Cort get out of the relationship? Were those two men up to something they didn't dare discuss with anybody else and, if they were, did it somehow connect with the missing Angela and Lucy Sumner? Surely Press wouldn't do anything to his own daughter!

She got up and found another beer, lifting the tab slowly. The worst question of all crept to the surface of her mind, like something turgid rising from a darkling sea: Was Cort finally becoming like his demon-possessed father, Georges Bellefontaine, the way that old devil had sworn he would?

Then she saw little Luke Simmons, unnoticed in the roomful of grownups, sitting on the arm of his father's chair. Quietly, Ellie saw, he was studying both Preston Sumner and her husband. The glint in the boy's eyes appeared surprisingly mature, inquiring, and . . . knowledgeable.

It was much later, the party at the Simmons' was over, and they were alone. Press and his nurse, Ethel Crawford.

The lights were blazing in the bedroom of the apartment he'd shared with Angela, and the young woman who had seemed so glacially cold was on her knees in front of the dentist.

It was easy, under these circumstances, to hold her gaze. It wasn't any problem at all. "Slowly," he cautioned her, eagerly staring, responding. "*Very, ve*-ry slowly."

Before the woman with the glazed eyes was finished he was already thinking, with anticipatory delight, about Tuesday. About his dear good friends Alan and Ginny. When he was through with them this time, Press knew, he wouldn't have to keep such a close watch on Ethel Crawford.

She'd do literally anything for him then. Any time. And so, the dentist realized, with such sudden excitement that he bucked forward, would any woman of his choice.

NINE

On Sunday, as usual, Alan read the morning *Star* from front to back. Occasionally he would find a classified ad offering a job at a newspaper in another Indiana city, or even at a paper in Chicago or Cincinnati. He'd cut it out, and spend the rest of the day brooding over the advisability of replying to it. But the truth of the matter was, Alan had spent all his life in the Stevenson and Indianapolis area and wasn't about to move to another city. He'd either make it in the newspaper business here or nowhere.

During the morning, Ginny read the sections of the *Star* that intrigued her, stopping now and then to clip an advertisement or coupon from some local store. Later, she tidied up around the apartment, looking to those things that she didn't really have time for during the week. That was one of the reasons she hated Sundays; she detested the housekeeping function of marriage. Monday through Friday and on alternate Saturdays, she had her part-time job at the photo kiosk to keep her mentally stimulated.

Alan, she knew from long experience, was the next thing to worthless around a house. It wasn't that he consciously avoided doing chores. He simply didn't realize they were there to be done, however obvious they were to Ginny. Worse, if she asked him to help, he was such a completely unmechanical as well as unphysical person that he tended to botch the job and require help inside of an hour.

All things considered, Ginny really preferred to do the chores herself and get them out of the way. It saved time in the long run. Besides, she had decided, it was really enough to have a husband who enjoyed spending all his leisure time with her. She'd seen enough of her supposedly better-off friends' marriages break up because the husband persisted in dropping everything to gallivant with his old cronies. A long while back, Ginny had decided that if her marriage ever failed, it would be over an issue of genuine importance—not sheets that required changing or garbage to be taken out.

There was also the fact that she knew, to her core, that she could trust Alan.

Around three o'clock, that Sunday, nine-year-old Luke came out of his own room, announcing that he'd finally read everything he wanted to read that day. The three of them gathered around the card table to play Monopoly. Luke won, as he very often did.

While the day might have been uninspired, even dull, it

THE DENTIST

was also peaceful and relaxing for Ginny. Without knowing it at all, it enabled her to prepare herself for events that were just over the horizon.

And which began, rather stunningly, the next morning.

Luke brought in the mail, riffling through it in a fruitless quest for a new catalogue from Johnson-Smith, the huge novelty company over in Michigan. In his rare, truly boyish moments Luke loved palm-buzzers and X-ray tubes and instructions in ventriloquism. But this time his hopes were dashed. All he found were bills for his parents from the Power & Light and gas companies, his father's September issue of *Ellery Queen's Mystery Magazine*, the autumn issue of *West Coast Review of Books*, and a surprising letter addressed to his mother.

Ginny rarely received letters, unless they were from Luke's grandmother, who lived in Arizona now. *This* envelope—the plain kind that came in a package at the local drugstore, the curious Luke observed—was addressed to "Ginny Simmons" in a handwriting he didn't know. He paused briefly, wondering what it would be like to call mom "Ginny," then held it up to the morning sunlight. Despite the way he squinted and manuevered the letter, he couldn't see much. He did note, though, that the postmark was dated a week earlier.

Luke didn't bother mentioning the fact to her when he handed Ginny the mail.

She tore the letter open.

Dear friend Ginny,

I am aware that friends worry about one another, and since we were becoming very close until the moment when I decided to leave Press, I am conceited enough to believe that you are concerned about me.

This is to let you know that both my little girl Lucy and I are okay. On the day we walked out, I stopped at the bank where Press and I had a joint account. Don't let him tell you that I cleaned him out because I didn't. I took half. I deserved that much.

It seems strange to warn you against believing Press, since it was only in recent weeks that he ever lied to me. But he has changed enormously, Gin, that's all I can tell you. What's going on, I simply do not know. The trouble all stems from *that man* (here the words were underscored several times in Angela's red ink) and what he has been doing to an ordinary little person like Press. I couldn't stand by and watch it happen, even though I do not know what they have in mind. I only know it is not decent, and may even be evil.

The breaking point for me came when I heard *that man* tell Press that each of us must make a "sacrifice" if we are to obtain what we want. That didn't sound right to me, Gin, it sounded sick somehow and I realized they were both beginning to frighten me. Because how could I know whether they'd decide that poor little Lucy or I might be the ones they wished to sacrifice?

That sounds terribly melodramatic, I know, even to me, but a woman must follow her own feelings and conscience in such matters. I will call you in a few days to give you my new address but it *must not* get into Press' hands or Cort's. I'd rather your husband didn't even know. I'm fine, as I said—really—and so is Lucy. I'd like to get back into interior decoration and plan to do so but I must take any job soon because the money won't last forever and I would really prefer

THE DENTIST

not to accept support or alimony from my ex-husband.
(Got to begin thinking of him *that way*!!) Rather earn
it on my own.

The letter was signed, in a quick, crimson scrawl, "Your
maybe foolish but constant friend, Angela."

Ginny sat down to think for a moment. She'd been dressing to get ready for her part-time job when Luke brought in the mail and her hair was still up in curlers. It was a gigantic relief to hear from Angela. But it was also obvious that Angela wasn't exactly A-1. Ginny shook her head. Clearly, the redhead was so mixed-up and confused by the changes in her life that she'd forgotten that she had already told Ginny where she and Lucy were staying. She looked at the letter again; it wasn't dated.

Or maybe, Ginny thought, maybe Angela meant that she was taking Lucy and moving to yet *another* new location. Yes, Ginny decided with a snap of the fingers, that was probably what she meant.

Ginny began taking the curlers out of her hair, a task Alan called "dismantling your head." Tomorrow she would visit Preston Sumner's office to have her tooth filled. Since Angela hadn't put an address on her letter, it wouldn't hurt Press to see it. She figured, as she plopped the curlers back into a box, that it would show him how independent Angela was trying to be. And Ginny would be able to tell from his reaction what he knew. That would complete her relief.

More than a week earlier her brain had begun making adjustments, dilating its own vessels and calling-in additional blood from storage chambers in the liver and long muscles. That had failed, and more dramatic chemical changes were initiated in the brain. Immense quantities of sugar were consumed. The cortex worked with haste, in higher frequencies of fast beta waves.

On the day he attacked, she sloughed off 500,000 million cells—but she'd lost that many every day of her life, the way we all do. Bacteria continued to swarm over and through her body, tastelessly immortal; thriving. If no white blood cells or viruses killed the bacteria, they would live forever.

Respiration stopped at the moment she struck the floor, and the complicated life-reporting network of brain activity vanished violently. Entirely normal, regular bloodflow was the one thing that might conceivably have saved her—if it had been achieved within six minutes.

It wasn't. Her killer did nothing to keep the bloodflow from slowing to a halt, and staining.

He only picked her up, and drove her *here*—several safe miles away—locking her out of sight and leaving her to rot.

In common with most people, he looked upon her remains as quelled, stopped forever. He did not know what an active process death could be, and usually was.

Within the first twenty hours after he'd murdered her, the pupils of her unseeing eyes dilated and then, surprisingly, contracted again. Subtle alteration, but scarcely nothing at all. The eyeballs themselves dropped, sank deeper in her head. Routine; important routine. Blood finally sank to feed the capillaries in the lower regions of her immobilized body, and her skin acquired the distinct pallor that most people notice in a fairskinned, dead human being. As biologist Lyall Watson observed in *The Romeo Error*, death is a procedure the way living is, or dying. *Things* remain to be done.

Approximately a dozen busy hours after her killer ended

THE DENTIST

the more obvious part of her life, her body attained rigor mortis. That meant that her muscle fibers began stiffening, from the intestines out to the muscles of her face.

But about one and one-half days later, the muscles relaxed, normalized again.

Incredibly enough, her liver went right on manufacturing glucose for a full three days after the murderer departed. The body gives up the fight grudgingly, one sweet inch at a time; her body fought hard for her.

Futilely, however, because no one knew where Angela's body was. Not that finding her remains would have made much difference; according to interpretation of clinical death around the civilized world, she had been dead since the moment he struck her.

Today, when Ginny came to the tentative conclusion that Angela was "all right," her lovely, long red hair and the nails of her hands and feet continued stubbornly to grow.

TEN

They were deep in the office; the glaring, revealing sun of that cloudless Tuesday morning had been left outside. "You're really concerned about Angela's whereabouts, aren't you?" Press inquired, calmly folding the letter his patient had given him and slipping it into his white jacket pocket. "You think she might be in some danger?"

Ginny nodded. She was sitting in the dental chair.

Dr. Preston Sumner continued looking steadily, sincerely down at her. The deep brown eyes behind his thick spectacles were compassionate, full of his obvious caring. Sympathetic. "Something inside of you," he said again, "tells you that she simply may not be . . . all right. But you have no real basis for fear?"

Again, Ginny nodded. Physically lower than he, staring up at the stocky dentist, she felt a little lightheaded and under the man's command. She felt no resentment, no resistance or struggle. It was all right, really; because every fiber of her mind and soul believed, today, in Press Sumner. Each time she met his somber gaze he seemed, like some enchanting and exotic flower, to reveal another soft leaf—one more intriguing layer that she had never sensed.

But even before she, Alan, and Luke arrived at the office on Tuesday—no work was scheduled for the boy, but he'd asked to come along—Ginny had confided in her husband that her "trust in Press, both as a member of the medical profession and as a friend and a person," seemed to be growing daily.

"That isn't a 'both', babe," Alan had said from behind the steering wheel, stalling with an old editorial technique. He'd forgotten his sunglasses and was squinting against the adamant morning shine. " 'Both' means two things, and you cited three. Member of the medical profession, friend, and person."

His lighthearted criticism had been distinctly jarring to her. She'd blinked and turned to frown at him, the late summer sun gilding the skin over her high cheekbones. "Don't tell me you don't feel it, too—different about Press— even if you are both men."

"That 'both' is okay," he had replied with a grin, refusing to meet her eyes. "Press and me; two."

He'd been actively stalling because her "trust in Press" was getting on his nerves, and he was male enough and reporter enough to be skeptical—so long as he could—about everybody and everything. Wholehearted commitment went against

The Dentist

his professional grain. Next thing he knew, Press would be running for mayor of Stevenson. Or for pastor of the high-steepled Methodist church.

And now that he had again experienced enormous pain in his friend's dental chair, and was waiting in lugubrious misery for Ginny's work to be done, he was damned if he was going to give the guy a blanket endorsement. Although, he thought with private honesty, that was pretty much what he'd done on Saturday night: seizing Press' plump paw and then thumping him on the back. Whether he admitted it or not, the truth of it was that whenever anybody was around the oral surgeon for more than an hour, these days, they were full of pleasantries and sentiment for good ole Press Sumner.

Shamefully irked by the fact that he wasn't hearing any shrieking yet from Ginny, he winked at Luke and made himself a personal pledge to check things out more fully. Maybe the guy was using some kind of drug to enhance his own popularity and sex appeal. Perhaps there was something in the history of dentistry that would serve as a clue.

In the inner office, Ginny was saying, "I like to assume that this letter from Angela means she's moved to another neighboring town." She paused, reddening. "I was about to tell you about your little girl's doll, but I don't want to repeat myself."

"I've known where Angela was since shortly after she left me."

It took a second to register, and then Ginny was gawking at him in surprise.

He smiled easily. "Nurse Crawford here chanced to run into Angela at a grocery store," he explained, "and naturally told me where she was. Both she and Lucy appeared quite well."

"But these—these charges Angela makes against you and Cort Devalyn," Ginny protested, bewildered now. "That you may be doing something terrible, even evil—that you talked about 'making sacrifices,' and that you'd begun lying to her . . ."

"She refers to 'that man,' " Press murmured, glancing at his beautiful assistant. "That could mean anybody, not necessarily Cort."

"Oh, yes!" Ginny said firmly, nodding. "She goes on to say—"

"It isn't exceptional for a wife to be jealous of her husband's friends, is it, Virginia?" the dentist asked. "Women can sometimes become so terribly possessive."

"That doesn't sound like Angela to me," Ginny answered desperately, turning her head to look at the dentist's aide. Ethel Crawford's eyes were red. She looked very ill at ease. "When was it you saw Angela and Lucy?"

The nurse's lashes batted twice, three times. "When was that, doctor?" she asked.

"About a week and a half ago," Press said smoothly, his eyes locked with Ethel's.

"About a week and a half ago," Ethel Crawford told Ginny obediently, as firmly as if she'd made the calculation herself. She began fastening a protective bib around the patient's pretty throat. "About a week and a half ago."

"Well, do you know where she is now?" Ginny demanded, baffled. "Is she still in Stevenson?"

Press glanced with seeming annoyance at his watch. "We really must get started." He drew near his patient with a magician's flair for distraction, quickly slipping the plastic cup over her mouth and nose before Ginny even knew it. "I don't want you concerned about Angela any longer, my dear, or about my little problems." His heavy lenses appeared to be fogging up above the apparatus pressed to her face, and the top of his head, from the forehead up, was elongating like some hydrocephalic skull. "So I think we'll just take care of all that and go on without any further fuss."

A clamp held Ginny's mouth open, just so. Her consciousness shifted to low gear and chugged down the darkened track of her conquered mind. Most of her teeth and gums were exposed now in a terrible, snarling expression that pressed one cheek against her eye, as if she were winking at the oral surgeon.

Preston Sumner had studied hard in dental school. He'd learned exactly where the nerves were and how to get to them, how to lay them bare like tender infants lying beneath a stamping jackboot. With the first, swift, dart of his drill he burrowed into the pink of her gum and smiled, warmly, when Ginny's shriek rose into the office like the final horrified scream of someone buried alive.

He had rendered the young brunette helplessly-unconscious—*but still able to experience pain.*

The next step was two-fold. The first phase was the administering of intentionally, professionally chosen exquisite pain in the overt guise of dental medicine. Filling the single cavity in her tooth, a while later, was duck soup. It would take only a moment—and it wasn't the other phase of the step. But this initial element, locating the predominantly sensitive nerves, and drilling directly into them without blinking an eye, was more challenging.

He glanced at Nurse Crawford and saw that he'd been

right. Now, for example, one of her full breasts was peeking unprofessionally from an unbuttoned gap in her uniform, but she neither noticed nor cared. It wouldn't be necessary to keep a literal eye on the woman any longer. She was his, totally, now, and Press squirmed a little at the thought. If he told her to strip and perform sex on him while yet he labored, she would do so without question. If he told her to seize a scalpel and slice her own jugular vein, Ethel Crawford wouldn't hesitate.

If he told her to kill Ginny Simmons where she half-sat, half-lay—and remembered, or forgot it—that, also, would happen. Press giggled. He was the only man he knew with a slave.

Now the dentist jabbed on the opposite side of the tooth, deep enough to draw a thin stream of blood, and he was rewarded by the most piercing scream of pain he'd heard yet. Although his own lips turned up in an appreciative smirk, Doc Sumner reminded himself that he was no sadist, that he wasn't doing this to the girl simply for amusement. Amusement was merely a plus. There was an practical reason for administering pain to his friends Ginny and Alan.

And it all went so very far back in history, to fifteen hundred and fifty years before Jesus Christ, when the Egyptian papyrus of Ebers was conceived. In it, Sumner knew now, there were intriguing passages tracing back *another* two thousand years—to 3700 B.C.—without the slightest mention made anywhere of dental extractions!

Now that, of course, was remarkable and, at first, confounding. Clearly, to Doc Sumner and the thin, smiling man who at that moment left the private room at the back to join him beside the writhing Ginny Simmons, it was obvious

The Dentist

that the ancient Egyptians *must* have pulled teeth, to relieve themselves of pain—unless, of course, there was some reason lost to antiquity for them not to do so. It had been the search for that reason that had brought the two men together.

In a few moments, now, the second phase of this next step toward fulfillment of the Plan would begin. That would be the province of Press' tall colleague.

But for now, the quest for magic lay in the dentist's adroit and skillful hands.

The first discovery had been that it was pain—blinding, intense, agonizing, exquisite pain—that made the world go round.

They should have known it all along, Doc Sumner felt. Humankind lived with pain from the moment of birth. Each being came into the world through a process of complex pain—the process of birth itself.

And when the new male or female was freed from that process, he or she was struck again, early and often. In childhood, there were diseases, falls and cuts, the beatings given by other children; in young adulthood there was the psychic pain of the whole racial demand to mate. By the time they were middleaged, male or female had been painfully inoculated, damaged in all manner of accidents, ill with racking pain or subjected to operations— medical and dental— more times than they cared to discuss. They'd been subjected to psychic pain from insults or grief. And they would end their lives on the globe in the agony of death.

But no one had seen it as clearly as Preston Sumner's friend, no one realized for a moment *what it all meant*:

It was pain that created every new turn in human life, that manipulated every significant alteration; and each individual's agony throughout history—since the days of the ancient Egyptians, and before—had been multiplied a million, NO, *a billion times*, steamrolling, gathering into itself, tumbling like a snowball down an infinite mountainside of anguish—until war was virtually a way of human life, in order to wreak the penultimate changes of humankind. Penultimate; because the ultimate, of course, was the jealous destruction of the world itself by those who had been subjected to so much pain that it could only be justified by the annihilation of All.

Most importantly, it meant that when pain became truly bad enough, when it was consciously inflicted—consciously and intentionally—it made the mouth itself spread wide and left open the pathway to the soul. The avenue of infinity, the boulevard of life, the highway to immediate capture and control of the human soul! For the "knowing person," as it was expressed three thousand years ago, painful penetration of the nerve-filled system through the mouth provided a means to seize and direct the soul—and rule mankind itself.

Press again drove the drill deep into Ginny's unprotected mouth, realizing that the Nazis, in their experimental programs under Hitler and Eichmann, must have intuited what they had in their hands. Why, the barren, etched woods round death camps must still be filled, he thought, with the terrible cacophony of psychic wailing—the song of eternity only he and his friend heard today. If ever the Big Bombs fell on all the world, raining hell's own thunder on every living thing simultaneously, crisping Life and aureating it, the skies themselves would split in sundered glory and deep from the kissing lips of earth would arise a blazing and tunneled passage—to Forever!

And only he and his wise friend, who would soon administer the *second* stage of commands, knew precisely what they meant to *do* with their arcane knowledge—only they knew what was *planned* for the souls they were so assiduously collecting.

When next the centered drill penetrated, Ginny Simmons found herself soaring into a garbled, garish, scarlet summit that left her breathless but mercifully without pain. Unaware of the sensation of motion at the apex of her soul's great vault, she found herself hovering, disembodied and alone. Far below her were the manifold forms of earthly agony. Formless, Ginny saw the drifting passages of infinite time like a moving stream eons below her, the bobbing heads of humankind mere drops in the endlessly shifting life-sea. Too high to hear the wails and protests, too low yet for paradise, she existed in an aerial absence of old realities and put out her tremorous psychic arms to embrace the new—

"There now," Preston Sumner said, rhythmically patting her cheeks, "That wasn't so bad, was it?"

Ginny blinked. Ginny opened her eyes and breathed. Ginny lived, residual pain returning on a flush of rocketfire in her offended mouth.

When she went out to the waiting room, collecting her purse and heading for the rest room, nine-year-old Luke stared at his mother in much the way he had, so recently, stared at his father and his friend Brian. This time he could not even ask her if she were all right before she disappeared into the ladies' room.

Alan hadn't spoken either. Taking small comfort in the fact that Press had finally furnished his wife with the gift of terrible pain, he told Luke to wait there for his mother and went outside to get the car. If she felt the way he did, she wouldn't be up to walking across the parking lot.

Luke's thoughts churned as he found himself alone. Was he next? Would they come for him? Doctor Sumner's inner door opened carefully, and Luke's unofficial uncle, lanky Cort Devalyn, peeped into the waiting room.

His gaze fell on Luke. He'd thought the Simmons family was gone by now. In a moment, he smiled at the lad. "I heard somewhere you want to be like old Uncle Press when you grow up," he ventured.

All Luke could see of the anthropology teacher his head floating more than six feet up the stretch of inner door. "I'm not sure about that any more," Luke murmured, barely above a whisper. Quickly he glanced out the front window to see if his father had pulled up. He wished mom would hurry. Finally he looked back at Cort and shook his tousled head decisively. "No, I don't want to do what Uncle Press does. There's too much pain in it—pain for nice people like my mom."

Cort's face was good-humored and easy now, all teacher and big brother adviser. "Sometimes, son," he said in his stout tenor, "pain is a means to other things. For example, people who cannot *feel* pain are often in awful danger, especially if they've broken something. Sometimes people must experience pain, for their good or even the good of others."

Then the head pulled back inside, turtle-like, and Luke stared where it had been.

There was no good to pain, he knew that. It didn't take a high IQ and good grades to know a dumb thing like that. Animals knew it; little tiny babies knew it. And that meant Uncle Cort was a liar, just as "painless" Uncle Press had

THE DENTIST

badly hurt his mother. It meant neither man was to be trusted.

Unshaped, childish loathing began to build in Luke Simmon's young and brilliant mind. With it came doubt, and hefty suspicion. And right behind them all came a new decision all Luke's own.

The decision to watch his "adopted uncles" very, very closely.

ELEVEN

Part of the drastic fall-out from drunkenness or narcotics—perhaps the very worst effect of all—is what happens to unknowing children.

Luke Simmons had never seen his mother and father incapable of dealing with normal household matters before, but neither of them had behaved normally since getting into the old Granada and driving home from Uncle Press' office. Dad had very nearly piled the car up, at the Pendleton Pike exit, and, when they entered the apartment complex, could only park with one wheel on the curb.

As the next two hours passed, Luke became increasingly terrified. Neither of his parents was able to read the headlines in the evening *News*; they giggled about it with good humor Luke found strange. When mom left her jacket and purse on the floor by the front door of the apartment, he blinked in wonderment.

Not that it was their fault, or that they didn't try to shake off the effects of the dentist's drugs.

But two people whom Luke loved and considered to be intelligent, competent people seemed to have been drastically changed to inefficient auto-atons by their visit to the office. And without any prior experience in dealing with the altered states of personality, Luke had no way of knowing that the effect was not permanent.

He perched on the edge of his chair at the dining table, staring first at Ginny and then at Alan. The meal she'd concocted was virtually inedible: scarcely-heated vegetable soup, warmed-over mashed potatoes and hamburgers, plus wilted salad that appeared to have been retrieved from the garbage. Mom had put chocolate syrup beside a carton of cottage cheese that was obviously on the turn, and provided stale rye bread for the shriveled hamburgers. Luke sipped the soup and tried not to look at the other dishes. For her part, Ginny looked straight ahead without eating or moving, her hair dangling in her pretty but vacant face.

Alan, did not touch a thing, but yawned every minute he was at the table. When his shirt cuff dangled in the chill vegetable soup, Alan didn't notice. "Whew, I can't seem to shake this feeling," he muttered several times, his words scarcely distinguishable between jaw-cracking yawns. To Luke's inexperienced ears, he sounded disgustingly drunk.

Finally Alan stood, ramrod straight, grunted "g'night," and headed for their bedroom. Ginny followed, promptly, managing a hideous smile at Luke before staggering down the short hallway.

"What about the dishes?" Luke called after them.

"They'll wait t'tomorrow," his mother said over her shoulder.

Luke huddled in a chair in front of the television set. Although the channel was turned to the public TV station, which was broadcasting a history of doll-making in the Orient, Luke didn't get up to change it. For the first time in his nine-and-a-half years he was afraid to disturb his mother and father.

From the groping shadows emerged the beautiful white-gowned body of a woman, and it was not until the crimson fires behind her illuminated the top portion of her body that Alan realized she had the head of a lioness.

Colored a tawny yellow with the furry ears laid back in watchfulness, the great cat's head contained the searing eyes of some creature as intelligent as man. He was almost sure they weren't really human being's eyes, set deep in the golden and powerful skull, because the intelligence—while high—appeared distinctly alien. There was an abysmal coldness to them that discounted his presence before her—her name, Alan knew all at once, was Hert-Ketit-S—minimizing it to the point that only some small need remained for him.

He could not recall ever feeling so insignificant, and so puny. The unknowable genius of those bizarre and frigid eyes had peered deep inside his own simple consciousness and found it wanting, and frail. He knew they had explored him for the simple reason that his own deepest thoughts, feelings, and needs felt used—violated. Worse, they were as nothing to the lion-headed goddess.

She snapped her fingers to some gamboling creature at her side. Raised to her on a vast, enpurpled pillow was the longest knife Alan had seen in his entire life. It looked too heavy for Hert-Ketit-S, but she grasped its hilt lovingly and raised it with uncanny ease. Alan swallowed hard. The point of the great knife dwindled to such razor sharpness when the leaping flames at the goddess's back flicked like lightning, it drew a clear *humming* sound from the vicious instrument.

Alan lifted his eyes to discover where it was he stood. The sheer cliff walls of some vast, subterranean pit rose on all sides to the height of redwoods, unclimbable. *Hatet*, the word hissed in his mind, bringing pain; *you shall dwell now in Hatet, in the eleventh section of Tuat, the underworld.* He nodded his head quickly in intuited obeisance; yes, yes, it was the hour before the final hour, it was indeed the Egyptian Hades governed with cruel and calculated injustice by the guardian-queen Hert-Ketit-S.

His eyes, pained and burning, leapt back to the she-being and saw that she had sinuously drawn near him. With her lion's gaze fixing his face, her woman's hands undraped the virginal white gown, presented herself to the mortal—

—And Alan screamed in his troubled sleep, seeing first the indescribable beauty of her golden breasts and golden pubis, seeing second the smouldering flames that began to jet from her body—violent, consuming fire that belched toward his shrinking humanness and singed his own form.

That was when she swung the enormous knife from right, to left, below waist level, *hacking* at him: and then he sat up in bed, his eyes great in fright, his mouth bawling a hideous shriek . . .

* * *

The Dentist

Vast and heavy, Ginny Simmons' belly rose from her bed like an impossible tumor. The swelling continued as she stared down at it, watching her small, inverted navel disappearing into the pregnant mass like the inturned lips of a monstrous balloon.

But she wasn't on her bed, she realized, and Alan wasn't beside her in sleep.

She lay instead on hot desert sand. In the distance, she could make out the shimmering outline of fresh-built, triangular structures stretching skyward: the pyramids themselves. She reclined on Egyptian sand at the dawn of civilization.

Ginny struggled to rise but her great abdomen continued to swell, marks of her tautness emblazoned in her naked flesh like the tracks of some insistent animal. Her efforts to stand stopped when she heard the sounds, to her right, and spun her terrified head to *see*.

The entity wore a towering headdress with the fixed and staring features of a vulture, its head topped by a glowing snow-white crown from which two brilliant feathers of some unknown bird lapped perpetual-summer's air as though tasting it. Below the headdress was the slender but big-bosomed body of the eternal female, concealing gauze wrapped round and round her sinuous shape as though in a cocoon from which Wonders might one day appear. Clutched in the right hand was a regal scepter formed like a long-stemmed crystal flower; and her left hand brandished aloft the mysterious enigma of an Egyptian *ankh*, its twists glittering beneath the bright sun like some jewel forgotten by time.

"I am Nekhebet," came a feathered voice from beneath the vulture headdress. "mother of mothers, father of fathers. Beneath my clothing lies the primeval abyss from which all light bursts forth, giving—or withdrawing—the life force. I am the symbol of what nature forgot, the patron of what nature must produce."

Now Ginny could not see over her grossly distended belly and she knew with certainty that she must soon deliver. When she attempted to answer Nekbehet, clots of red blood tumbled from her lips but were caught by the steaming air and turned to small, sweet buds. *What do you want of me?* her mind cried. *Why am I here?*

"To have your child, my dear," the she-thing replied, and unwound her garment of gauze.

Ginny gaped impotently at the soaring enormity of her bosom and then at the huge thing springing well below it—an impossible phallus rising like a pale and tumescent sun from the apex of her slender legs—and she screamed in terror. Without pause Nekhebet removed the vulture headdress, revealing the true feathered head of a living and genuine vulture, its great beak drooling rivulets of blood. Feeling movement, Ginny peered down that instant at the child beginning to crawl from her own belly. At the sight of the monstrosity emerging to view, scaled and multi-legged, she threw back her weeping face in a shriek—

And the two Simmons, Ginny and Alan, side-by-side in their bed, stared in heart-thumping panic at one another.

"Oh, my God," they said as one, falling into one another's arms.

Moments later, frightfully weak but clear-headed at last, Ginny got out of bed to check her son Luke.

She found him in the front room, curled up in his father's chair asleep. Across the way a snowstorm was happening on the screen. Public television had long since shut down for the night.

For a moment Ginny did not awaken the boy. She slumped to the carpeted floor at his feet, leaning against the chair and sighing her confusion and despair. "Why does everything feel so wrong," she whispered to herself, in the dark, "when there is really nothing at all to point to—nothing to identify as the start of something truly frightening?"

Because Ginny could see nothing had happened to make her so terrified. On the surface, life was no different than it had been a year or even a month ago.

Young Luke heard her troubled whisper and came to. For an instant he stared at her, scared, unsure whether it was really his mother who sat near him or that bizarre creature he remembered from the dinner table.

"Mom, mom," he said when he was sure, reaching down to hug her. His arms went gladly around her neck and her dark hair tickled his nose with joy "Mom, mom . . ."

Finally she held him at length, smiling at him through the shadows. "I was just a little sick, Lukey," she told him, "from the anesthetic Uncle Press gave me. I'm okay now."

"And Dad?" the boy pressed with eagerness. "Is he—himself?"

Ginny thought of Alan's face when he awakened from the nightmare. "Of course," she said, wondering if it was true.

She fixed cocoa for the two of them and they sat on chairs in the kitchen, talking the way they had in the past.

Until Luke asked her a question: "Mom, did Uncle Press know where Aunt Angela is? Does he know if she's safe?"

Slowly, a perplexed expression crossed Ginny's face. She frowned as she sipped cocoa from her mug. "I'm really not sure what you mean, honey," she told the boy. "Aunt Angela simply went somewhere else to live." She paused, looking curiously at him and failing to distinguish a certain *clicking* sound deep in her ordered mind. "Why wouldn't she be safe?"

TWELVE

Before Alan Simmons left for work, he was careful to assure his wife that she had little to be worried about. Yes, it was true that he'd also felt "things" were in some manner vaguely wrong recently. But that could be attributed to the fact that he'd hated turning thirty in June, and Ginny was dreading her thirtieth birthday in November. The mind tended to play funny tricks, if you fretted about silly things like that. Besides, he said, turning thirty—and forty, sixty, seventy-five or ninety—appeared to beat the only alternative!

As for each of them awakening in the middle of the night, screaming from the worst nightmares either of them ever had, that was undoubtedly because Press had used the same drug on each of them. It might have been something new, without all the kinks worked out. Next time, they'd simply insist upon a different anesthetic, and everything would be fine. After all, they'd had plenty of bad dreams in the past, and undoubtedly would have more in the future.

He finished by pointing out what a smart boy they had and how much they enjoyed the apartment, the town, and their friends. Then he got into his car and drove two miles to the paper—without believing for a single minute anything he'd said to Ginny.

Truth of the matter was, Alan had been getting increasingly concerned about the undercurrent of secrecy in Stevenson lately and he was smart enough to know that they had something to do with Press Sumner and maybe Cort Devalyn, Alan's old friend.

Unlike Ginny, Alan had not been hypnotized in order to forget this growing anxiety over Press's missing wife, Angela. Sometimes a man develops concerns faster on his own without his wife goading him, he thought as the boxy one-story frame building came into view. Just because he didn't talk about them all the time or go off half-cocked didn't mean that he lacked simple compassion. After all, he'd read the letter from Angela. He'd seen one or two other overwrought letters from women who were divorcing their mates, and they didn't have an undercurrent of stark terror of the husbands they were leaving.

None of which meant, Alan mused as he nodded morning's greetings to other newsfolk and wended his way back to his cubbyhole, that Press had actually done a thing to Angela. It was enough that she was terrified. For all he knew, she might need a capable psychiatrist and yet, there she was out there on her own, somewhere, with nobody near to lend a helping hand. Hell, the little girl might even be in danger.

But not, he imagined, from Press. Either of them. The dentist was such a nice guy he'd even called up this morning, first thing, to make sure Alan and Ginny were all right. Hardly the actions of a guy with a lot of complicated or sinister secrets he'd planned to spring on the woman he loved!

The logical thing, he decided over a cup of coffee at his desk, was to try to figure out what Press was into that Angela could have misinterpreted. And since both the dentist and Cort Devalyn kept haranguing everybody about the history of dentistry, and mythology, the smart place to start was clear as a bell.

He shouted in for Perry Olson, the red-haired and freckled copy boy, to get his ass over there. Perry came running. While the kid waited, Alan carefully scribbled a list of books and topics he wanted Perry to check at Hoosier Subject's brand-new million-dollar-plus library. The library had been assembled as the result of a bequest set up in the will of Phoebe Gregson Huddleston, widow of the man who had founded the paper thirty years earlier, and it had been the answer to Alan's prayers several times.

Then he watched Perry hustle away. Thoughtfully, Alan licked the corner of his mouth. With just a little luck, he might get a line on what had frightened Angela Sumner, and that might possibly suggest where she'd gone. Additionally, the information might help eliminate some of the budding fear. Not Ginny's, particularly: his own.

* * *

Ginny was wearing a robe over her underwear, running the sweeper in the dining alcove, when she heard the sharp rapping at the door. When she went to it and peered through the peephole to identify the caller, she could scarcely believe her eyes. A smile spread across her face.

Press Sumner stood on the other side of the door, grinning happily—hand-in-hand with little Lucy.

Ginny ripped the door open, dropping happily to her knees in the same motion to tuck the five-year-old against her bosom. "Sweetheart!" she cried, hugging her and then holding her at arm's length to look at her. "Where in the world have you been?"

The dentist raised his stubby index finger to his lips, clearly cautioning Ginny. He said evenly, "Apparently she's been at a baby sitter's in Indianapolis most of the time. I received a phone call from the woman, a pleasant middle-aged person named Marti Planner, saying that no one had come back for Lucy. Reluctant to turn her over to the authorities with all the traumatizing things that would have meant for Lucy, she finally pieced together her real name and the fact that she lived in Stevenson. If it had been Indianapolis, with hundreds of people named Sumner, Mrs. Planner never would have found me."

Lucy looked well, adorable in a jumper which highlighted her red hair. Ginny looked back up at Press. Meaningfully. "Could we leave Lucy with some ice cream in the dining room while we talk out here?" He nodded, and Ginny plumped the girl into Luke's chair and then brought her a big bowl of Lindner's chocolate ice cream drowning in syrup and whipped cream.

Breathless, she sat opposite the dentist in the front room.

THE DENTIST

"I don't understand all this. Where in the world is Angela? I thought the two of them left together."

Press spread his hands. "I don't know." He caught a breath. "Candidly, Virginia, I think my wife was having a nervous breakdown. For all I know, she's caught a plane to New York, forgetting all about her child."

"Oh, Press!" Ginny reached for him, holding his hands in hers and looking heartbreakingly sympathetic. "You poor guy! There's nothing worse in the world than a runaway mother. A child Lucy's age *belongs* with a woman."

"Precisely my thinking," Press replied with a sad nod. He smoothed his hair back, proud of the way the bald spot had vanished, and sighed heavily. "Knowing how close you were to Angela, and to Lucy, I thought, perhaps, that I might impose—only for a short while, of course, until I can make other arrangements."

"You want me to keep Lucy?" Ginny blinked, suddenly abstracted and peculiarly dizzy. In her mind's eye she saw her naked stomach swelling before her. *Mother of mothers, father of fathers. I am the symbol of what nature forgot.* "I'm not sure what Luke would think, of course, and he's still so young himself." Pain caught a muscle just inside her eardrum in a vise-like squeeze. *To have your child, my dear.* "Perhaps, for a while, we could . . ." Her gaze dropped between Press' legs, saw the way his genitals pressed against the material. She blinked as pain lanced both temples. "All right, Press, I'll take care of Lucy a while. In fact, I'll be delighted!" Abruptly the pain and confusion were gone.

The dentist's brown eyes danced before her face. "Don't worry about Angela any longer," he said softly, taking her hand again. "Do you hear me? Don't worry about her."

"Of course," she said, just as softly, oddly moved by the man, oddly moved in other ways that she could never mention to her husband Alan, "Of course."

When he had gone, Ginny went out to the dining table and took a chair next to the tiny redhead. Lucy looked up at her, tears standing in the vivid blue eyes. "Where's mama?" she asked plaintively. "Where's my mama?"

"Sh-h, darling." Ginny hushed her, patting her arm and fighting back a terrible psychic impression of entrapment, of rape. "Everything will be fine."

When she looked at the bottle of syrup on the table, she thought for a moment that the image of a vulture appeared in the sticky dark brown substance.

When young Perry brought him the books, Alan gave him a grin that swiftly became an unexpected surge of headache pain jolting its way through his ruined jaw. Beneath his lids were flames of crimson, and he imagined that he could almost make out a human shape behind them.

He took three aspirin with a swallow of his ancient morning coffee, shuddering, and dug into the literature Perry'd brought.

There were plenty of superstitions involving teeth, that was obvious. In Australia the two lower incisors were knocked out, by tribesmen using wooden wedges and a stone; they were thought to have magical properties. Teeth were often worn as a talisman in Europe and the Americas. In some places, a woman felt that she'd have no uterine trouble if her child's first tooth was pulled and worn at her waist. Certain Africans believed that teeth yanked from a human skull cured migraine and toothache as well. And the teeth of an executed

The Dentist

criminal, once they were pulverized, were felt to be excellent for the restoration of virility.

Magical properties, Alan was still trying to blink away the pain in his jaw. *Talisman. Restoration of virility.* It was all absurd, of course, a collection of old wives' tales. But what *would* a man do to banish pain; to have command of others; to be sexually vigorous again?

He scanned more of the books Perry'd brought to him. A child's milk teeth, he read, might be used for sorcery if they fell into the wrong shaman's hands. Alan looked up, staring into the newspaper's single massive copy room without seeing it. A vision of his son Luke jerked in front of his eyes, Luke with string extruding from his lips. Luke, and a dollar bill and darkness. Alan gripped his temples with his hands and concentrated. What had happened to those teeth he'd pulled for the kid? Did he *really* remember getting them, and leaving a dollar—*no*, a ten-dollar bill!—under Luke's pillow? Or was that what he'd intended to do?

And if he had gone into Luke's room to get the child's pulled teeth, did he throw them away—*or what*?

I'm reading too much of this superstitious nonsense, Alan concluded, shoving the book away and reaching for another. He'd see what the old encyclopedia said about dentistry. A little fact for a change. . . .

What Cort Devalyn and Press Sumner, not to mention his own Luke, had said on the topic appeared to be true. Accurate. It was Aesculapius who first extracted teeth, Herodotus who urged the specialization of dentistry, Hippocrates who—as they said—connected teeth to longevity.

Again Alan hesitated, tapping the page. Hippocrates was the name invoked even today, revered by every new physician.

What if the old boy had been right, twenty-two hundred years ago? Was there any chance that one's teeth *did* influence how long one lived?

Not until 1000 A.D. did someone try to remove tar and other substances from teeth, one Abul Kasim, an Arab. Gabriel Fallopius (1523–1562), an Italian anatomist, described uterine dental development; Antony van Leeuwenhoek analyzed the form of tartar from teeth a hundred years later; and Pierre Fauchard, a few years after that, became known as the founder of modern scientific dentistry.

All of which was getting him nowhere, Alan decided, as he read on. You could, he saw, diagnose pernicious anemia and blood dyscrasias from studying the teeth—whatever "dyscrasias" meant. Cretinism, pituitary ailments, syphillis and Addison's disease were all sometimes observable by peering into the old yawp.

He was closing the history book when he saw the paragraphs related to the papyrus of Ebers. For the first time he learned there'd been no reference to dental extractions in the then-current papers, in 1550 B.C., nor any that had been done all the way back to 3700 B.C. And, like Cort Devalyn before him, the newspaper man wondered why not. It didn't seem to make any sense at all—unless *magical* sense in a way he, Alan, could not determine.

But perhaps Cort, the anthropology teacher and professional student, *could*.

Cort did a great deal of research, always had. He subscribed to everything, it seemed, was in constant touch with dealers in antiquarian books and antique objects everywhere in the world. So for the sake of argument—Alan pinched the bridge of his nose, trying to block out the recurrent pain—

what if Cort, with his queer love of the past, had wondered why *there'd been no extractions in the past and succeeded in obtaining bizarre, arcane papers that gave him the answer? And what if the answer opened Cort's road to discoveries that were* beyond *other modern men, secrets of greater virility, improved health, maybe even cures for dread diseases—genuine* magic *that could be used to get others to do things against their will?*

It sounded absurd—but down deep inside, Alan had always wondered about his old friend Cort's private ideas, secret ways. When they'd been kids in high school, Alan remembered Cort driving a junker and parking it in alleys, hoping to see women—any women at all—undress at night. Yet he'd claimed that they didn't arouse him, that it was "sheer scientific curiosity." There'd been a time when Cort could have had almost any girl in class, but he had looked loftily down at them, not even luring them on—and had then astounded everybody by becoming serious about chunky, ordinary little Ellie Parks Devalyn! When Alan asked him why, Cort had replied: "I am interested in how people react, what they want, how they behave when they get it. Ellie is so damned grateful, Alan—and besides," Alan could still see the acne-marked young face, calm as death in the shadows of the old '53 Chevy, "they're all constructed the same way. What difference does it really make in the long run?"

That, yes, *that* was the reason of his old pal Cort, Alan realized now. It wasn't that he was wrong about his information—he was unfailingly correct—but that he saw the *uses* of information differently, and never quite found the data he needed. Needed for what? Alan took two more aspirin.

Needed to set him free, he realized, getting excited despite himself. Because even then, during his high-school years, there had been something about Cort that was haunted, tied to something that he wanted to escape—*had* to escape—even when he appeared most eager to learn more about it. Alan sighed. Cort was a man who got his facts straight and then went *all the way with them*, anxious to unearth fresh data, unexpected reactions! And he couldn't remember a time Cort hadn't been willing to use the facts he acquired in any interesting way he could invent to do so.

Alan picked the book up nervously, glanced at it, then placed it next to the others.

If it was even remotely possible that there were complex, esoteric, even evil secrets in Egyptology—whether they hurt other people or not; whether they hurt *himself* or not—it was brilliant, odd, lonely and enigmatic Cort Devalyn who would pry them out and put them to work.

Whatever it took to be set free.

It had surprised Luke Simmons to learn that Lucy would be staying with them for a while, but he was determined not to get jealous.

Sitting alone in his bedroom, only dimly conscious of the fresh anger welling up inside him, he glared at the late-afternoon gloom creeping across his venetian blinds and tried to get stoic. Why should a guy be jealous of some little-bitty *girl* creature with long red hair? Just as long as she stayed out of his books and his games, and didn't mark all over his homework, they'd get along all right.

But there were some matters going on around him that he couldn't really figure out. The girl, Lucy, for example. The longer the day became, the more he began to feel a measure of genuine sympathy for her. It was obvious to anyone who

The Dentist

could think with their minds as well as feel with their emotions that either Cort Devalyn or her own father had done something to Lucy's mother, Aunt Angela. Killed her, probably.

What disturbed Luke was trying to see *why*. The former "uncle" Cort was a lot like him, a thinker, a man who laid his plans carefully. And unless Luke missed his guess, Press Sumner was right in the palm of Cort Devalyn's hand. Obviously, it wasn't the dentist who did it to Angela—"offed her," the guys at school were calling it—because he didn't have that kind of guts. He probably just let Cort handle it, or arranged it for him.

The question was plaguing incisive, methodical Luke to no end. Cort wouldn't off the lady just for fun; no, there'd have to be a lot better reason than that. Not necessarily anything to gain, like money in the mystery stories Luke read sometimes, but for some kind of—of intellectual reward.

Well, tonight would be as good a time as any.

That night, when Cort and Ellie Devalyn and their children went to bed, a small, silent, figure watched with binoculars from half a block away.

A guy could never tell what he might learn.

THIRTEEN

Cort had insisted on sexual relations twice already that early-August night and Ellie, floating in perspiration, had cooperated as she always did—not without surprise when the second time came around. While it had been true, in their marriage, that the anthropologist tended to experience peaks and valleys of desire—clustering his demands for days at a time, then refusing to touch her for months—the only time they'd ever shared sex twice in the same night was on their honeymoon. He'd been curious about the sensation of a different position. When she had sought his attention a third time, he'd bolted into the other room of their hotel suite and finished their first married night alone in a chair. Uncommunicative and staring.

Wide awake after the second occasion, this night, Ellie wondered what had aroused Cort's passions. She felt absolutely certain it wasn't some thigh-flashing senior out to get a good grade from summer school, or another member of the Von Braun faculty. One female body, he'd told her several times in the past, presumably meaning to be reassuring, was as good as the next; so why chase? He'd added, to her astonishment, that a girl in puberty or a senile old woman would serve the need, "assuming that either was physiologically and psychologically competent."

Ellie wasn't even certain that what they'd been doing tonight was having sex, whatever it might have seemed to be on the surface. Court had a keen edge of excitement that he couldn't express in words—or wouldn't—but communicated with every electrical touch and sudden movement. She felt that he might have been trying to bank his energies, or redirect them. Certainly they weren't making love; the very euphemism annoyed Ellie increasingly as the years went by. For some people, she supposed, warmth and consideration and a mutal adoration entered into it; but Cort's cool, efficient, somewhat analytical approach to sexuality had turned her off more than a decade ago, and it still did.

In fairness, he'd explained the way he felt about it all when they were in high school and Brian was illicitly conceived. "Sexuality is a relatively unreasonable urge imposed upon us by nature along with the lesser animals, and its demands must be served, not so much to continue the race—which is an arguable motive from a logical viewpoint—as to be intellectually freed to follow more interesting matters without interference. Done properly, of course, like most animalistic activity, it isn't without transient pleasure." She could still

The Dentist

remember how awed she was by Cort then, on every level, and by the fact that he'd chosen her.

Resentment didn't set in until rather later, and by then, she knew enough about his past—and the truly diabolical father from whom he'd been taken as a boy—to engage her sympathies for him without requiring his appreciation in return. She'd seen Cort, for years now, as a paternal construct who could be geared up differently by a considerate, compassionate woman. It wasn't until he became involved with that dentist, Press Sumner, that Ellie realized she had been hopelessly wrong.

In all fairness, too, she sometimes found him marvelous in bed. She reminded herself, again, that it was all right to feel like a wanton and care nothing about the man as a human being. Looking over at his naked body now, as he lay absolutely still, Ellie wished she could take him for what he was, once and for all. Like most Aquarians, he was tall, without an extra ounce of weight anywhere. Even his chin, despite the way it was tucked in this moment, remained singular, not pluralistic. His stamina and endurance, in sex, were remarkable considering how little he exercised and how little obvious musculature he possessed. Her eyes fell to his flat belly and then to the thin but generous length of his penis. Ellie knew it lengthened very little when he was erect but thickened, both at the root and at the corona, almost as if he controlled it and wouldn't permit any excessive show. Indeed, Cort knew how to use what he had, the penis, the hands, the lips and tongue, give him that. So why wasn't his efficiency satisfactory after all these years?

Why did she still hunger for a part of him she could not

have, and which, she confessed sadly to herself, might not even exist?

"You're concerned about me, aren't you?"

He'd asked the question out of the blue, without turning his head. His lips had moved a bit, in one of those queer little smiles he had at times; but not his head. But his gaze was no longer blank, fixed on some crucial inquiry; the eyes were keen again, reflective but present.

"I am, sometimes, when I don't know what you're doing," she said softly. Her mouth felt slightly sore from where he had shoved against her. "And you are doing *something* with Press Sumner. Don't deny it."

He ignored her remark. "I was thinking about those parts of my childhood that I blanked out," he said amiably. "They've been coming to mind a great deal recently." Now he did turn his head to look at her. "Slowly but surely, I'm remembering every bit of it. Don't you think that's healthy?"

Ellie snuggled against his hairless chest and kissed his jaw. "We've talked about that before, honey. I don't honestly know." She hesitated, unsure how he'd take her next remark. "When George Bellefontaine is completely lost in your memory, as if he'd never existed, you've made your best accomplishments—and I think you've been happiest. But when you remember the man, well, we've had problems then."

"But Georges Bellefontaine was my father," he answered simply. His breath was oddly minty near her cheek. "Nothing can alter that, really. And he was willing to sacrifice me—take my life, himself—for what he believed in."

"You've remembered that?" Ellie asked, not knowing that her nails dug into his arm, below the shoulder. "That's all come back to you?"

The Dentist

Cort nodded. "I know what you and my foster parents tried to do, keeping the details from me. It was for my own good. But now, well, I've felt it all come back—and it's all right."

"You were so *little*," Ellie argued gently, pushing herself up on her elbow. Her breasts looked perfectly round, the way everything about the blonde seemed rounded. "I don't know how you can deal with such a dreadful thing as your own father trying to murder you."

He sat up, pulled the sheets over his long legs. "Don't you see, Ellie, *that's* the part that's all right." His gaze returned to her, feverish. "I *understand* why he had to sacrifice something he loved. Honey, I don't even blame him!"

Ellie didn't reply for a long moment. She lit a More menthol and puffed quietly on it, frowning, tapping the small, fine ash into her bedside ashtray. "I've never been your equal intellectually, Cort, and I never will be. I've let you make every key decision in our life together, because it was common sense to allow the smarter person to make them." Abruptly there were tears in her eyes. "But I—I have to express my opinion that *not everything* can be . . . intellectually justified, rationalized! It's okay for you to understand that Georges Bellefontaine was a monster who could kill his flesh-and-blood for some—some unguessable reason. But I *don't* believe, not for a moment, that it's okay to say what he did might be all right. Such a thing could *never* be all right!"

The bedside lamp provided the only illumination in the room and it flickered then, as Cort's eyes flashed lightning. For an instant she almost thought they glowed. "You've properly identified the distinction between us, quite nicely," he said coldly. "You aren't especially bright, my dear." He saw her flinch away from him, hurt. "Don't look that way! I simply spoke the truth—agreed with your own estimate of our respective intelligences. Ellie, damn your simplicity, it is conceivable for there to exist a reason for *anything* that might occur! Anything at all! It is the emotional fools of the world, functioning on nothing more than their animal feelings, who make such a mess of human life. But a man who seizes control of his own existence, accurately evaluates it, balances his plans against the stupid exigencies or customs around him, may be intellectually justified in *any act at all*!"

"I don't believe that for a moment," she managed, blinking beneath his fervid stare. "Senseless wars, innocent people killed by drunken fools, teenagers out of their minds on dope, harmless children battered insensible—"

When he turned quickly toward her, Ellie jumped. But he was only moving to take and hold her hands, to move his long, eager face closer to hers. "Don't you see, El, *those* are the acts of emotionally unevolved people—of the kind of fools I was describing? Why, *we* aren't in disagreement! Any living beings hurt for no reason at all represent a terrible waste."

Ellie stared back at him, mystified but less frightened.

"If I kill the governor of this state tonight," he said, trying hard to explain, "on a whim—because I hate authority figures—I should be executed by the end of the week. I will have functioned on emotional impulse, worse, on my own weakness. But if the governor is a dangerous man in his position, if he is actually like those fools we were discussing, and I kill him"—Cort dropped her hands to spread his own, smiling happily—"why, I should get a medal! I have behaved rationally, for a sound purpose!"

The Dentist

Ellie put her cigarette out, her head averted. She sighed. "Oh, Cort, I just can't follow that. Maybe you're right . . ."

"If you could grasp the distinction," he said, his voice barely more than a whisper, "I might be able to tell you what Press and I are doing."

She looked at him sadly, shaking her head. "I don't lie to you, Cort. I only know you tell me that you remember being pinned-down by a hideous man who was your father, surrounded by naked witches, threatened within an inch of your life by a knife with which that madman meant to kill you—and you're saying it was acceptable. To be honest, the fact that you can do that scares the hell out of me."

Suddenly he shoved her back to the mattress, threw one leg across her body, and straddled her. "I'll tell you this much," he said, rubbing himself against her. His long face was twisted with secret purpose and an unswerving obstinacy that she'd never before seen. Although it was a hot summer night, Cort's skin was dry, even rough to the touch. Crouched over her, he lowered his voice to a husky whisper and his breath was no longer minty—it stank. "*Listen* to me, Ellie, because it's absolutely marvelous! I'm trying to do the *same* thing that my father Georges Bellefontaine tried to do, when he saw a crucial part of the formula. And the only difference in the world between our plans is simply that *I know how to do it*!"

He laughed. Incredibly, he was erect again—but now his penis *was* longer, startling and immense in its new tumescence. Ellie was dry when he forced himself into her, and it hurt.

But it didn't hurt nearly as much as it hurt her to know, even in general terms, why her husband had been so passionate tonight.

When he exploded hotly in her, with his fingers dug deep into the soft flesh of her buttocks, Ellie prayed that she'd never know exactly what it was Cort and Press were trying to do.

A small boy standing on a rise in the street adjusted his black binoculars. He gasped and gaped.

Circularly framed in the lenses before his eyes, Luke Simmons saw the lifting, looming shadows of Cort Devalyn in intercourse. For a tick of the clock his naked, thrusting figure was stunning to the youth because of what he was doing.

Something extraordinary happened then.

The shadowed figure of the anthropology teacher he'd called "Uncle Cort" looked momentarily . . . *winged* . . . with two projections leaping into binocular view, one on either side of the man's head.

That might have been nothing but a trick of the lighting—the lamp inside the apartment in concert with the passing automobile beams outside, and the streetlamp nearby.

Then the whole window filled with a searing red light, but for the rise-and-fall of the tall, thin man, who remained a nightbird etched in stony black.

Luke took one, two steps away, lowering the binoculars, scrubbing at his eyes with his knuckles. Images streaked past his inner eye—pictures of destruction, devastation, and an undead Force that would not *stay* dead. Staggering, almost falling, the nine-year-old glanced one last time with his naked eye at the crimson haze, at the plunging ebon form of the winged man—

The Dentist

And knew, without a doubt left in his head, that he stood within range of evil, murder, and death.

Luke turned and ran for home.

Like Alan Simmons, Cort Devalyn dreamed of Tuat, the Egyptian underworld, and knew even while he slept that he was seeing the place from which *It* would come—come for *him*.

Tuat lay in another dimension of the sky, divided into twelve sections, or nomes, corresponding to the hours of the night. And each one of them—which Preston Sumner did not know, because Cort believed he did not *need* to know—was ruled not only by an earthly, powerful nome-governor but by a vast number of fierce, unspeakable beasts—devils, whose contorted and ghastly countenances alone could warp the simple mind of the human ruler. Even now, in his dreams, the tall teacher saw the fantastic river running through Tuat, its pace at once rapid and rabid, *churning* with hatred and fear.

Soon, he sensed with a shudder, *It* would be here. He knew that because he had summoned It. It was needed.

Moments later, Ellie awakened and arose, fumbling in the darkness for her robe. Cort stared at her. He liked doing that, watching people when they did not know he was watching. Glimpses of large nipples, the breasts swinging heavily like pendulums telling time; fat, generous buttocks, his own red nailprints still streaking them, budding them with caked jewels of blood. Then she was gone from the room and Cort was sitting up in bed, instantly alert, attuned, except that a recent, recurrent headache had returned.

Without a need for motion, he looked off into the corner

of his bedroom, thinking. He'd like to have told Ellie the whole plan, because, in his own way, he loved her. *No*, Cort amended it; he *appreciated* her. She was like the car a busy man always needed. After all, one did not mistrust his automobile, he even cherished it.

The initial, key part of the plan had been the sacrifice, of course. Several weeks ago he'd begun to piece it together in his own mind and that had enabled him to enlist the dentist. Until then, until the moment when the influence of Georges Bellefontaine again throbbed in the teacher's thoughts, he hadn't been able to proceed. But then he'd dredged up his father's attempt on his life and seen the wisdom, the sweet *necessity* of it.

Two men were required, and each of them was obliged to sacrifice the life of someone they loved; then, when all the intermediate steps were taken, the two of them had to act similarly—in concert.

Because it was Press himself who suggested that his sacrifice be Angela, his lovely and talented redhaired wife, Cort's actual taking of her life had been acceptable. It was evidence, after all, that Cort was in charge, that Press was obedient to his will.

And down the road lay Cort's own *personal* sacrifice, a road that was running short now. Already they were on the outskirts, nearly prepared to reach the golden city. Cort felt perspiration break out on his forehead for the first time that night; excitement rolled in the blood of his veins. But now the personal sacrifice had to be slightly different, not fast the way it had been with Angela.

As it had almost been with Alan and Ginny Simmons, it would be necessary for the sacrifices to be achieved at the outermost

The Dentist

limits of excruciating pain—*sacrifices that genuinely hurt him and Press, pain that* created *death, and opened the passageway to that which Cort Devalyn sought above all else:* Personal immortality. Eternal life.

"Where have you been?"

Luke had thrown his binoculars into the closet as he dashed through the front door of the apartment and ran into the dining alcove. There they all were, waiting for him. It was mom who asked the question, obviously frightened. It was dad whose face was crimson with indignation and looking at his wristwatch. It was Lucy Sumner who stared at him, a chocolate pudding mustache prominent on her upper lip.

But it was Lake who made himself stop before he blurted it out, shouted the warning at them the way that had worked on his lips all the way from the Devalyns' street.

Instead, gasping to catch his breath, the nine-year-old swallowed the words whole: *Mom—Dad—somebody's going to die!*

FOURTEEN

As things turned out, Cort Devalyn, Press Sumner, and Alan Simmons weren't the only people in Stevenson, Indiana, doing important research that summer.

Ellie Devalyn had been keeping busy, too. She had begun a considerable time ago, without quite knowing what it would lead to, and then largely forgotten about it.

Until early in August, when she received two meaningful packages—one through the regular postal system, one by way of United Parcel Service—which provided her with a great deal of startling information.

Both of them concerned her troubled husband's flesh-and-blood father, the late Georges Bellefontaine.

One parcel contained a magazine which Ellie studied with fascination and revulsion. In it, nearly thirty years ago, someone calling himself "Rupert Coven" had written an article about the famous practitioner of black magic. The other parcel had been harder to get. She had found it necessary to contact a slow-moving back-issue-newspaper clipping service for it. But now the packet of photocopied press stories had arrived. They had been written at the time of Bellefontaine's remarkable death.

The former had been one of those dozens of unfortunate periodicals which are no longer in print. Unlike *Colliers*, *Liberty*, *Mystery Monthly*, or *The Saint*, Ellie didn't have to wonder why the magazine had failed. It deserved to.

With a garish cover depicting a battalion or two of hell's fiends virtually swimming in flames, entitled *Visions of Hereafter*, the magazine was a strange amalgam indeed. On one hand there were letters from something called Brotherhood of the Archangel, a group of robed-and-hooded people attuned to the pulse of "the Hierarchy." These "letters" were chockfull of do-gooding suggestions for living well, interspersed with references to a UFO bearing Intergalactic Brothers, through which the Hierarchy communicated with the Brotherhood. Or something. Ellie's nose wrinkled as she turned the pages.

On the other hand, however, there were articles with vaguely complimentary remarks about *wicca*, which Ellie quickly learned was witchcraft. The article about Georges Bellefontaine was similarly praising in tone; and reading the piece, Ellie couldn't figure out why:

The Dentist

Gatherings of naked people who were sometimes asked to share sexual relations might seem, to the world at large, nothing more than an orgy. To Bellefontaine and his devoted followers, however, a sound theological purpose lay behind every groan of ecstasy. He explained it to *Visions of Hereafter* in a recent exclusive interview.

"Just as we know that pain may, if it is intense enough and properly induced, open the pathway so that we may enter that which is infinite," he declaimed, pressing his long fingers together and looking at us with those disturbing, dark eyes, "intense pleasure can open the pathway for the infinite to enter *into* the seeker. It is a question of direction, Mr. Coven, whether one is trying to go to the Source, or ask the Hierarchy to come in."

"You are saying, Doctor Bellefontaine" (Ellie paused, annoyed; since when was that old fraud "doctor" *anything*?) "that the initiate seeking the Hereafter must concern himself with sheerly physical phenomena, like mouths, teeth, lungs? That going to the infinite powers, what you have termed 'the pathway,' is physiologically mechanistic?"

Bellefontaine nodded emphatically. "Whether one can see it or not, the soul has a distinct location or site. The problem with searchers throughout history is that they have assumed nature must turn against her own laws in order to accommodate good and evil, that it willingly permits the breaking of physical laws. Nothing could be further from the truth, Mr. Coven. It is why all religious people, be they adherents of what we call 'God' or what we call 'Satan,' sometimes are disappointed by an apparent failure of the deities to respond. Those we worship and who govern nature rarely, if ever, take steps which work *against* the nature that they created themselves!"

I paused to consider what Doctor Bellefontaine was saying. "What does it take, then, to get an answer to one's prayers?"

The mage smiled. "If one asks questions of He whom we call 'God' in anger, jealousy, or fear, his purely physical brain is not equipped to receive a reply. *That* would be the logical provence of Another, would it not? In order to know any deity, to contact the Archangel or those beings who have especial interest to me in the pursuit of Egyptian cosmology, it is a matter of knowing how to manipulate *actual corporeal substances of nature*, whether inanimate objects from forests and mountains to food substances and air itself, or animate objects such as human beings ourselves."

Ellie set the magazine aside for a moment, brooding. Why was it that this concept sounded entirely plausible to her, when it was the idea of a madman—an evil, certifiable killer?

Then she remembered what she had learned through her own study of astrology, years ago. Interesting, worthwhile ideas—even elements of truth—could come from any source at all, including one's small children. Brilliant professors, like Cort, did not have a title to the truth. It was free and, she mused, a question of license in the lifestyle of people like Georges Bellefontaine.

Delving further into the strange article, the little blonde learned that "Doctor" Bellefontaine bragged of how he was rearing his "my only son, Cort Bellefontaine" in his own "apprehension of the realities." It wasn't until she reached the final pages of the piece that she was truly shocked, however.

"I am pleased to announce to your readers," the tall and aristocratic Bellefontaine continued, "that I have given my son Cort to evil. The pledge is made, it is unbreakable, and everyone around me expects great things from the boy one day."

For those of you who are new to *Visions of Hereafter*, our editorial concept is that there are two primary paths to what we choose to call the Hierarchy. They are neither divisible nor, individually, is one superior to the other. Each shares with the other an impatience with the mundane matters of man and an appreciation that our time here is temporary, at best, fundamentally made important only to the degree that we find our own "pathways" to the divine.

But Georges Bellefontaine is the first subject of an interview in these pages to be entirely candid about his position. For those who have heard about his formal sacrifices, conducted with only minor precautions against outsiders, and rumors that lives have been taken in the noble cause he espouses, Doctor Bellefontaine's acute honesty will come as less surprising. Still, we wondered (on behalf of you, the reader) how he can be so sure that his infant son will follow in his own impressive footsteps.

"Simple," he answered the question with a booming laugh. He tugged his black cape around his wide shoulders, then reached down to stroke the partly clad, mute blonde woman at his feet. "I have paid a sizeable price, quite willingly, to guarantee it. The price, by the way, is my obligation to *return* to this world many years after my passing—something few initiates care to do, once they have reached the other side of their choice. This arrangement, Mr. Coven, means that my little son Cort will be watched, assisted, and guided at *every* stage of his life."

"How?"

His eyes blazed. "I have procured for him . . . a guardian demon."

Ellie closed the magazine with a heavy sigh, shaking her head. Internally, she felt a tremor start. As it was in all Satanic elements of faith the concept of a "guardian demon" was a blasphemous twisting of the original. Whether it was true—whether a person could actively, literally be observed and guided by some foul, devious monstrosity—Ellie didn't know. She didn't want to, either.

Reading the articles about Bellefontaine's death took less time since, most of the clippings she had been sent contained the same information: A neighbor on Georges Bellefontaine's street had finally had enough when she heard whispered rumors that a child was scheduled to die. She telephoned the police. On the basis of what her complaint they were able to obtain a search warrant and break the door of the shaman's apartment down.

"I don't guess I'll ever forget, what I saw in there," an officer named R. D. Duncan testified at the trial. "Mostly they were these ladies, almost naked, dancin' and moanin' as they circled some kind of altar. A few of them was lyin' in the corner, though, doin' things with some men who was there too. A lot of mathematical designs was written on the floor, both in chalk and in blood." Apparently Officer Duncan had been asked a question at that point. He continued, "The blood was from these two teenage children who'd been hung by their ankles from the ceiling, dead when we got there. Well, Bellefontaine was at the center of everything, standin' over a naked little boy. He couldn't have been more'n three or four years old, a skinny kid, scared out of his wits. This Bellefontaine wore a cape but he didn't have nothin' on under it. When we busted the door in, he had a huge knife over the little boy and I shouted at him to drop it. Instead, he turned on me, mad as hell, and lunged. That was when I and Riley put two bullets into him. Yes, he kept comin' and we kept shootin'. Finally he dropped down at our feet, bleedin' like a fountain."

My God, Ellie whispered, reaching for a cigarette and lighting it with fumbling fingers.

"Crazy thing was," Officer Duncan's thirty-year-old testimony finished, "whilst I was untyin' the little boy, two things happened. First off, ole Bellefontaine actually *gets up* to his knees, gore drippin' outta his mouth and nose, and by-God threatens us! 'You haven't heard the last of Georges Bellefontaine,' he gasped, red bubbles on his cracked lips, 'because he lives on in Cort, my son.' Which was when this teeny boy gets down from the altar, runnin' to his father who'd wanted t'kill him. He wasn't in time—Bellefontaine fell forward on his face—

but the kid looks up at us, his eyes just like Bellefontaine's, kind-of wild-like, and says clear as a bell: 'You'll pay for this. The whole world will pay for this!' Frankly, I think the kid needs a good shellackin' and then some decent folks to raise him right and git all that nonsense out of his head."

The court had agreed. The little boy had been reared by the Devalyns, a middle-aged couple who had badly wanted children. The little boy *had* been decent, like them, at least until he began to remember his terrible start in life. She shook her head and put her research in a drawer, locking it.

That was nine days after Luke Simmons thought he saw something evil in the apartment of Cort and Ellie Devalyn.

On the tenth day, in the afternoon, all the Simmons' friends joined them in the complex clubhouse to celebrate Luke's tenth birthday.

In addition to the four Devalyn children, the Grazells' baby and Lucy Sumner, who was still residing with Luke and his parents, the new ten-year-old had asked his friends from the complex. It was a sober party, except for a single beer consumed outside the back door by each of the fathers. It wasn't until after the gifts were opened and Ginny had served ice cream and cake that things settled down enough for conversation.

No one had noticed how carefully Luke steered clear of his former "uncles," Cort and Press, nor how he had watched their behavior around his Lucy.

The other mothers, with the exception of the hostess, who really preferred male companionship, were out by the bar in the second room, keeping their attention on the children. Lanky Cort was in the front room seated between Alan and Ginny on a couch across from the unlit fireplace, dressed in walking shorts, a white pullover sweater with huge pockets, and a sports jacket. Occasionally he touched one temple as if suffering from a headache. Press Sumner and Dennis Grazell were in chairs nearby. Alan, relaxed and anxious for a flash of Cort's old wit, puffed air through his lips and then smiled. "I don't know how you stand it with four of them, Cort," he offered. "You must be a man of steel."

"I'm no Superman," said the anthropologist, glancing at Alan. "But I take my fatherhood very seriously."

"That's a real conversation-killer," Alan replied with a grin. "What's got into you these past few weeks, Cortland?" He looked at Press and young Dennis. "Isn't he getting a little stuffy these days, men? Tell me the truth!"

"I'm sure he has a lot on his mind," the dentist suggested. Press had donned a tanktop and shorts for the occasion and resembled a Cub Scout who'd wandered into the wrong party. His full head of hair, however, was blowdried and fluffy above his freshly charming smile.

"It's *summer vacation* at Von Braun, for God's sake!" Alan declared, nudging Cort with his elbow. "What kind of hours are you putting in, buddy? Two hours a day? Three?"

Ginny saw the glint in Cort's eyes. "Alan," she whispered.

"No, dammit," he said, as startled as anybody by the anger welling up inside, "I'm sick and tired of the secrets being kept around here! I thought we were all *friends*!"

"We are," Press put in placatingly, "the *best* of friends."

Alan paid no attention. His quarrel was with Cort. "If

you're really working your butt off on something important, Devalyn, we can keep your goddamn secret, you know. Unless, of course, we aren't in*tell*igent enough to understand!"

Cort looked at him, his eyes glistening strangely. The newspaperman blinked, unable to sustain the gaze. "Situations change as we get older, Alan," he said softly. "We can't remain high-school chums forever, you know." He paused. "Someone once said that we all become our own fathers in time. That's why history repeats itself for most of humanity, but why, in addition, progress happens at all! Because certain great men have those sons who supplant them."

Alan got to his feet, his fists clenching and unclenching. Ginny gaped at him. "Well, all I gotta say, Cort, the old bastard *you're* supplanting must have been a weird kind of character! What was he, Cort, some mad scientist or something?"

"Take that back!" Cort was standing now, too, the color flushed from his narrow cheeks by anger. From the other room, Ellie heard him and turned, frightened. Most of the children were frozen in surprise, but Luke came forward slowly. "My father was a genius, Simmons, a man who let nothing get in his way! He provided me with a singular, glorious path to destiny. A destiny you'd never understand if you lived a thousand years!"

"You egotistical son-of-a-bitch, you smartass blowhard," Alan cried, beside himself now. "I'm fed up with that fucking superior attitude of yours. What are you anyway—a teacher? It's the teachers who've loused everything up for years, who care more about their paychecks than making sure our children learn how to read and write!"

THE DENTIST

"Alan, old pal, let's calm down a little, all right?"

It was Press, tugging at his arm. To Alan it appeared that the dentist was defending Cort, that he'd suddenly become alone in the world. Mixed in, too, were feelings Alan couldn't put into words: the loss of his own valued friendship with Cort to a man whom he'd once loathed. The old feeling of disgust he'd felt for Press flared. "Stay out of this, you little creep!" he exclaimed and swung his elbow, hard.

It caught Preston Sumner high on the shoulder and sent him spinning, fighting to regain his balance. Somewhere a little boy's voice cheered. But at that moment, Cort, redfaced, found unwise words rushing to his lips: "You can't do this to us!" he screamed. "Somebody mortal like you can't hurt us!" Furious, he swung clumsily at Alan with his right fist.

Alan, who hadn't been in a fight since the first grade, easily blocked the punch. In the process of throwing up his own arms in defense, he inadvertently shoved Cort Devalyn in the chest.

The teacher stumbled away, his long arms waving like a bird in flight. He fell to his knees, heavily, shouting with pain.

Something fell from one of the large pockets of his white pullover. Something that might have been a small purse, or pouch.

Luke moved with alacrity to pounce on it. "No-o-o," Press Sumner squealed, scrambling to his feet too late.

Color returned to Cort's face and to his eyes. Luke, staring at him, saw a psychological mask slip over the teacher's face, watched as the smile came to his fleshless lips. Then Cort was on his feet, casually brushing his knees, limping a little as he came toward the boy. Luke backed away.

183

"Give it back, son," Cort said as lightly as he could. "All right?"

"What is it?" Luke demanded. He held it behind his back. Now he had put the sofa between him and the teacher. "Tell us what's in it!"

Cort stopped. He turned to Alan although his gaze flicked back to Luke, and the pouch. "Man, I'm sorry," he said with vast heartiness, extending his hand. "That whole, silly thing was my fault. I've had these headaches lately, you see, and I've always been touchy on the subject of my father." He noticed that Ellie was in the room now, her mouth a grim slash. "Isn't that right, darling?"

"You've been touchy about a helluva lot of things recently, Cort," she said.

"There, see?" Cort said, as if she had verified his weakness. He turned back to Luke. "Give me the pouch, Luke, it isn't a plaything."

"I gave up playthings when I was nine," the ten-year-old said. He chanced a look away from the teacher, tugging at the mouth of the pouch, trying to open it. "What is this thing, anyway?"

Cort grabbed Alan's hand, wrung it. "Let's forget all this jazz, Alan, all right?" He was perspiring freely but his tone of voice sounded entirely sincere. "We've been friends since God was in diapers, remember?"

His gaze flickered back to Luke, who almost had the pouch open now but who continued to watch Cort Devalyn with the utmost wariness. "Dad, don't listen to him," he said slowly, his heart thumping heavily. "I don't think he's your pal any more. I think he's—"

Press Sumner, who had worked his way close to the birthday boy, darted forward.

Then he had the pouch in his own hands and was closing it, smiling nervously at the gathering. Young Dennis Grazell, he saw, was frowning, putting his arm around Mary as if to protect her. Suddenly Press held the pouch aloft. "I don't see why we should be ashamed of this," he said loudly, drawing everyone's attention. The strange, hypnotic set of his smiling lips created a growing ambience of trustworthiness and charm. "Shall I tell them what it is, Cort?" he called.

Cort's eyes blinked exactly once. "Why not?" he asked, shrugging.

"It is a talisman my friend Cort and I have assembled," the dentist announced, waving the pouch about like an auctioneer, or an old-time medicine salesman. "A wondrous, *mag-i-cal* talisman!" He matched the inflections of a barker perfectly as he beamed at them. "With this talisman, ladies and gentlemen, history records that a man can live forever! Would you *believe* such a thing? Live pos-i-tively *forever*!"

Then he laughed and tossed it ten feet to Cort. Cort caught it, put it back in his pullover pocket. "For the small price of one *thin* dime," he said, echoing Press' mannerisms, "you, too, can experience the thrill of *im*-mor-tality!"

Despite himself, Alan was amused. He found himself beginning to laugh. His lips pressed together in both embarrassment and an appreciation of the absurdity of his friends, he laughed harder, his shoulders shaking.

Then they were all laughing, delighted with the impromptu show. Dennis Grazell smiled gladly and murmured,

"Good ole Press!" Someone else took it up. Someone else said heartily, "Good ole Cort!"

Small Luke Simmons, solemn-faced, looked unbelievingly at the tableau, then turned, unnoticed, and ran out the clubhouse door toward the Simmons apartment. It was starting to rain but he scarcely noticed.

"I'm sorry, guys," Alan said softly, throwing his arms around their necks and hugging his old pals. "Maybe you aren't the only ones around here getting old and serious as shit!"

"Forget it, Alan," Cort told him, clumsily patting his chest and grinning.

"Everything's fine, old pal," Press assured him from the other side, hugging Alan back.

Ellie looked at Ginny. Ginny looked away.

They were in the men's room. The dentist shoved a heavy, sand-filled cigarette urn against the door, than sat on it. "Make sure it's all right, for God's sake," he said urgently, softly.

Cort was already opening the pouch, peering avidly inside. "It's okay," he replied with a sigh. "No leaks or anything."

Above them, the light in the ceiling glowed intermittently, bathing the room in yellow. When next it flashed the contents of the pouch were fully visible: pulverized human teeth—three crushed teeth that had grown in the mouth of an unborn child; and of course, the teeth of those who, like their friend Alan Simmons, had experienced precisely the right kind of intense pain.

"You know, I wasn't sure I was up to the sacrifices before

now," Cort said, slipping the talisman back into his pullover pocket, buttoning it this time. "Your wife was one thing, but *children*—well, they seemed like a different matter."

Press nodded as he moved the heavy urn away from the door and adjusted his mesmeric smile. "Don't worry. "We'll do that brat together."

FIFTEEN

"Can you show me just what it looked like?"

It was getting late that evening, and it was so humid that Ginny unbuttoned her blouse lower than usual, the top of her breasts freckled with tiny drops of perspiration. Father and son had removed their shirts; each of them appeared thin and frail to the woman who fed them. All three sat at the dining table. Lucy Sumner was already asleep. Now Luke nodded and accepted the pencil his father handed him, beginning to sketch, conscious of his parents' stares.

For more than an hour Luke had insisted that there were peculiar things going on, even if his father badly wanted to stay friends with Uncle Press and Uncle Cort. The boy got nowhere until it occurred to him to mention the pouch that had fallen from Cort Devalyn's pocket. On it, he explained to his father and mother, there were a distinguishing characteristic—a clearly discernible design.

He worked laboriously, carefully, for another few moments, light from the overhead chandelier spilling on his paper. *I don't want this to be*, Alan thought, frowning; *I don't want to believe they're doing something terrible.*

Luke stopped, laying his pencil down. He raised the sheet of paper, considering it silently. Finally he passed it across the table to his father.

"This is it?" Alan asked tonelessly, pointing. "This is what you saw on the pouch Uncle Cort dropped?"

"He's not my uncle any more and neither is that mean dentist," Luke corrected him, making a face. "I don't need family that bad." He nodded. "Yep, that's exactly what I saw on the bag. Only I don't think that's what it is. I think it's what the Egyptians called a talisman, just like they said."

Alan moved the paper sideways so that Ginny could see.

Luke had drawn the torso of a powerful man and, in the center of his chest, the part of sketch that Luke had spent the most time on, a crescent moon and disk.

"I remember seeing something like this in the research I did at work," the newspaperman said, studying his son's face. "It was something very important to the ancient Egyptians."

Ginny didn't answer for a moment. Then she touched his arm. "Apparently it's very important to Cort and Press, too. Did you bring your notes home?"

Alan nodded. "Hold on a moment, both of you."

He arose and went to his sports jacket, hanging in the

closet, put his hand in the inside pocket and pulled out a packet of papers. He sat back down at the table and, for a long, reflective instant, looked deep into Luke's eyes.

It shouldn't be hard for a man to choose between his son and his friends, but in matters of adult belief another ingredient was added to the stew—the extent to which children might lie in order to get even or to have their own way. Additionally, a small boy didn't always see just what he thought he did. His views were clouded by emotion, Alan thought, by an imagination that living in the real world hadn't yet placed in perspective.

But Luke was his only son and he was an exceptional one. His IQ was unquestionably many points higher than his father's. Who could know to what the boy might know that lesser human beings never suspected? And while Luke might not, in his specialness, be the kind of son Alan had once craved, although the lad sometimes made Alan feel that he was hanging-onto his own traditional superiority by his fingernails, the fact remained that he loved Luke.

That everything Alan thought right and proper *demanded* that he love him.

He sighed, began looking through his notes and finally found it. "Here it is."

Luke and Ginny craned their necks to see.

Beneath Alan's fingertip was a drawing he had copied from one of the books. The sketch Luke had just drawn might have been a Xerox copy of it.

"What is it?" Ginny whispered.

"It appears to be a representation of the Egyptian god *Thoth*," Alan read with care, his gaze flickering toward Luke. "He sometimes appears in the united crowns of the South and

North of Egypt, as well as in the fabled Atef crown." Now he looked darkly, even questioningly, at his wife and only son. "Thoth was their reckoner of time and seasons. If I interpret it correctly, Thoth was said to control time—to make of it what he pleased."

Ginny put her arm around Luke's shoulders protectively. "What does it mean?" she asked quietly, "that a design like that is on a—a talisman in Cort's pocket?"

Alan didn't answer. He stared out the window and saw that it was night now. There were crickets just outside, making the eternal music strummed by their ugly bent legs. If all the crickets in the world chose to gather in dark, swaying clumps outside the window, their perpetual and complex noise a means of planning an attack—to begin their war on mankind here, in Alan Simmons' home—he would never know it. He would see them only as crickets, to the extent that he could see them at all; familiar things that had always been around and which a man took for granted.

Like old friendships. "I don't know," he told Ginny at last. "Unless it means that Cort and Press have figured out a way, themselves, to control time in some way. To live longer, perhaps, or in a different time." He looked steadily at his son. "To make of life what they please."

"*Again*," Cort ordered hoarsely, reaching out with surprising strength to turn Ellie on her face.

She felt him behind her, on top of her, no longer making any attempt to be gentle or tender. When he forced his entry she cried out in pain, her weeping face smashed against the pillow.

It was the eighth time since they'd come home and she was

exhausted, sore every inch of her body. It was as if he had made a businesslike catalogue of the different ways to have sexual intercourse and was checking them off, one at a time, performing all the most debasing and painful positions first.

Originally she had felt that he surely must tire out rapidly, and she'd promised herself that she would make no effort to assist him, to get him up again. But that hadn't been necessary at all. It was as if his maleness had become a hard, relentless piston, something mechanical that would only erode to uselessness with the passage of years. Even now, he was still erect, glistening with moisture and traces of her own blood. It seemed to her then that Cort was on fire with lust tonight—not simple, sexual need and certainly not romantic desire, but a rutting lust that was less animalistic than automaton-like.

Except that he continually made *sounds* as he rose and fell, awful little noises that were half-chant, half-grunt. She'd never heard anything like them before. And, when she had been facing him, she'd been terrified by the glazed look of his eyes and the way that saliva formed on his lips and dropped, unnoticed.

This time, perhaps because they had never done it that way before, he'd finished quickly and tumbled onto his back, gasping for breath. Certainly he could not lie on his stomach without injuring himself. Painfully turning herself on her side, Ellie realized with a tremor that Cort might actually kill himself in the process of fulfilling whatever yearning possessed him. She discovered with rather little surprise that she didn't care much if he did.

The way he had turned her into an object was humiliating, and she knew it would prove impossible for her ever to forgive him. Whether she could love him again, aside from sexual intercourse, she didn't know.

She peered through her puffy eyes at him, lying there, completely ignoring her, thinking how like masturbation it was, in a way, for him to attack her this way, thinking, too, that he did not any longer look entirely like affable, scholarly Cort Devalyn. His muscles seemed oddly bunched and tight, except for those of the lower jaw which were slack, almost vacuous.

A shiver of fear passed over her rounded body. Was this, then, the way *Cort Bellefontaine* looked? Was it possible for a man to become possessed by *himself*, by the person he had been *meant* to become?

"What did you mean, at Alan and Ginny's party, when you got mad and told him he couldn't do that to you—that he was mortal and had no right to say such things?"

Ellie had asked the question without thinking about it, without even realizing that she was going to speak.

Cort's head turned toward her, the eyes golden in the light from their lamp, the slack jaw muscles tightening as he regained control. "I thought you understood that, Ellie, without any need for me to explain," he said in tones that were simultaneously quietly restrained and ominous—ominous, and oddly accented. Perhaps it was only that he'd worn himself out. "I really thought you grasped *that* much."

She hesitated, nibbling her already-tender lower lip. "So I'm dumb," she said, at last. "Tell me in English."

"It's simple enough, darling," he answered, smiling. "Beginning in three days, I'm going to live forever."

* * *

Ginny's legs released him, slipping down the sides of his body until they were relaxed on the damp mattress. "Shortie," she said, holding his face between her hands and kissing him a final time, "you are something else!"

Ritualistically, he lowered his head to kiss the tip of each nipple. Then Alan pulled out of her, smiling like a schoolboy who'd gotten by with something, and flopped on his side near her. "So are you," he said fervently, surprised by how little control he had of his voice. It trembled with joy and depletion.

"I wonder if anybody else is as happy as we are," she whispered, groping behind her head for her cigarettes.

"I hope so," he said magnanimously, getting her lighter and flicking it. It was one of the relatively expensive things he'd managed to buy for her and it had her initials. He knew she'd have killed to keep it. "But I wouldn't bet on it."

She watched smoke drift toward the ceiling. A reflective expression crossed her pretty face. "What are we going to do about Cort and Press?"

"You mean like go to the police?" he asked. The idea hadn't even occurred to him. "I don't see how we can. What have they done that's illegal?"

"I know," she said ruefully, offering him a drag of her cigarette. "The only thing we know for sure is that Angela took off. Left Lucy behind. And that's *her* crime—if it is one, legally. Not theirs."

He felt tired now, oddly dreamy. "I know something else, too, but I'd never be able to prove it. Press has changed."

"For the better," she said quickly.

He looked intently at her. "He's changed in a way that's

not quite . . . normal. The hair, for example. What the hell has he done to make his hair grow back in?"

Ginny shrugged. Just talking about Press this way made her unaccountably uneasy. "A secret transplant, maybe. We can't even be sure it isn't a wig, can we? But there's nothing wrong with a guy trying to *improve* himself, is there?"

He didn't reply at once. "Not if he's not hurting somebody else in the process," Alan said at last, reaching up to turn off the light. "I'm probably crazy, but I'm beginning to believe—"

A sound of scurrying footsteps outside the door. It opened.

Lucy Sumner stood in the doorway, only for a moment, then rushed toward their bed and threw herself between them, crying.

"Baby," Ginny cooed, comforting the little girl, "what is it?"

"Luke," she got it out, gasping, "Luke was gone—somewheres. Somewheres awful! He—he's cryin', too, 'cause he's scared."

Alan was sitting up, stroking the curls at the back of her head. "Darling, we won't let anything hurt you or Luke, I promise. Really!" He felt her lean back against him, the sobs starting to dwindle away. Alan took her chin gently and turned her face to see his. "My goodness, Lucy, whatever were you and Luke crying about anyway?"

The little redhead's face puckered in fresh terror. "Luke says—Luke says—one of us is going to *die!*"

SIXTEEN

There is a considerable difference between ranking a restaurant as the finest one in Los Agneles, say, or New Orleans, and claiming that one is the finest in Stevenson, Indiana. But the intent and expectations are similar, and when one goes to the best, wherever he happens to be, it may at least be said that he's spending top dollar and deserves a good time.

That was what Doctor Preston Sumner believed, anyway. It was two days before he and Cort Devalyn meant to culminate their long-standing plans. Partly for immediate thrills and partly to learn what he might expect of the marvels begun in his own office, the short and stocky dentist chose to experiment with his charm—and the pretty girls of Stevenson.

What he forgot was the difference between a genuine man of the world and a newly charming man who understood none of the finer points of the game.

Press asked seven different beauties to have lunch with him at Sol Greenburg's steakhouse. He told them, ahead of time, what's more, about the others who would be present. Each of them was to meet him there, rather than being picked up—in what the dentist chose to call "my private booth"—at precisely 12:30 o'clock.

Astoundingly, that part of the idea worked. All were present by 12:40. The one who was ten minutes late, a languid and southernly natural blonde who'd once been Miss Georgia State Fair, was peremptorily asked to leave. "If you can't be on time, the way the rest of us are," he told the gorgeous thing with newfound arrogance, "why, you'll just have to miss out on the fun." And he waved his fingers in a gesture of dismissal, unaware that two hours later, when his mesmeric charm wore off, Miss G.S.F. would count herself fortunate and wonder why she'd gone at all.

Working at appearing masterful, genuinely swelling with ego's gift of command, among other things, Doc Sumner sat as tall as he could in the booth at Greenburg's and surveyed the remaining half-dozen beauties with an eye that mightn't grow jaundiced for another few months. One or two of them he'd known as patients; another was a friend of Nurse Ethel Crawford (who hadn't been invited and languished in her home); and he had stopped others on the quiet streets of Stevenson just to see what would happen. The result in all six cases was the same. For reasons they would never after understand, Press Sumner looked to them like the most desirable man they'd ever met.

The Dentist

Press ordered boldly for each of them, dipping into a largely unexplored imagination to match their individual beauties to the delicacies of the afternoon menu. Each lovely girl, as he completed ordering, giggled or laughed, blushed or thanked him with fluttering, fetching lashes. As the meal itself proceeded, the dentist periodically reached beneath the table to squeeze, pinch, prod or grope, always to the enchantment of the pretty recipient. Emboldened, during a sumptuous round of desserts, Press caressed bosoms on two occasions when the other patrons weren't watching. Then he made the mistake of proposing to one woman that she join him in his bed at two-thirty P.M.

Unfortunately, perhaps, that was when he went too far. Immediately, the neglected beauties turned tigress, infuriated that he would see something in another woman which he hadn't observed in them. One, whose part-time profession happened to be go-go-dancing, suggested that he take them all to his apartment.

That ruined everything. Aside from the fact that Press seriously doubted his capacity to handle a half-dozen women, none of them was willing to share him. An argument quickly broke out with such clearly imminent hair-pulling and instant cursing that the dentist sneakily paid the bill and scuttled off by himself. Being arrested wasn't his idea of enjoying the initial gifts of immortality.

The more amusing features of the afternoon escaped him completely as he drove the streets of the town recklessly, careening around corners, convincing himself that he not only needed a woman badly but clearly had one coming. Consequently, he was not surprised when he found himself parking in front of the apartment occupied by one Ginny Simmons.

He knew that Alan would be at work, and he was reasonably sure that his partner's hypnotic efforts of recent weeks would still prove effective. If they didn't, why, his own special charms should turn the trick.

"Press! What a nice surprise." Ginny threw the door open warmly and waved him inside. It was a hot summer afternoon and she was wearing an old shirt of Alan's plus a pair of brown shorts. She was barefoot, and barelegged; Press suspected that she was wearing nothing at all under the frayed white shirt. He smiled as he followed her. "I just put your daughter down for her nap so we can visit in peace and quiet."

An idea occurred to the dentist. Instead of taking the seat on the sofa which Ginny offered him, he stopped at the entrance to the corridor leading to the bedrooms, exceedingly solemn. He'd worn his best suit for the failed luncheon and looked the youthful picture of a successful, serious man. "Could I just peek in on her, Virginia?" he asked. "I miss my little girl so badly."

"Of course!" She was on her feet promptly, leading the way to Luke's room, where they'd had to put little Lucy on a rented cot. The boy, she knew, was out playing somewhere. "There's your little darling," she whispered.

Press looked down at his daughter with the respectful attitude of a man in a mortuary. Her long, red hair was fanned in naturally beautiful display across a snowy pillow, and she was fast asleep. In Lucy, Press' rather snubbed nose had become an engaging stub. Her eyes, closed in rest, revealed violet lids so thin and fragile it seemed that she must be able to see through them. A sheet was pulled up to her neck, but one small arm had escaped and was outflung in innocence. To her father's suprise, tears came into his own eyes for a moment.

The moment did not prevent him from reaching out a hand to take Ginny's. "She is a beautiful child, isn't she?" He saw his friend nod. "There's so much of her mother in her."

Ginny, surprised that he had taken her hand, glanced at him . "It will be awfully hard to let her go. Alan and Luke and I have become very attached to her."

"You're a kind-hearted woman, Virginia." The dentist turned to her, inches away, moving his hand lightly up her arm and staring into her green eyes. "I wish Angela had been more like you."

Ginny tried to pull free and found that both his hands were on her shoulders now, gripping her tightly. "We're all stuck with being who we are, I guess."

"Luke's bed isn't being used." He was concentrating hard on her now, attempting to draw her across the room with him. "I've always been so fond of you."

Ginny opened her eyes, startled that they'd been shut. It was so *hot* here! She shook her head a little, aware that she had taken a step toward the man without realizing it. Somehow her mind felt dulled, deadened; despite a dim realization of what Press Sumner was doing, she had an overwhelming urge to lie down, to sleep. She twisted her wrists and found that her hands were pinioned by his. "Press, let me go!"

"Oh, you don't want me to let you go," he said softly, trying to lock his gaze to hers. "Do you?"

She shook her head. When she finally understood the question, she nodded several times, firmly. "Oh, yes, I do—I want you to let me go!" *Alan*, she thought, *I mustn't do this to Alan*. "Please . . ."

"But I can't, Virginia, don't you see?" He had her at the edge of Luke's bed, and they were sitting down as if it were the most natural thing in the world to do. "You want me. You realize what a nice man I am, don't you?" He saw her nod, blindly, her lips parted. "You realize how desirable I've become, how much you *need* for me to make love to you. Don't you?"

Her head was swimming. The room had tilted, there was almost no air in it, she felt that she might burn up. What was he saying? She nodded, half-politely, half to make him be quiet so she could think. His hands were on her shirtfront now, she knew, and that shouldn't be allowed—should it? *Where are you, Alan? Alan, I need you!* Was Press still talking and was he the one who was making her so dizzy? Now he was unbuttoning her shirt, only it was really Alan's shirt so maybe that was all right; because it wasn't actually bad for one man to see another man without his shirt, and right that moment Ginny wasn't even sure she was present— she might simply be asleep, dreaming these crazy things . . .

Press slipped the shirt off her arms, biting his lip in excitement. He had been right. She hadn't worn a thing under it. Her breasts were lovely, the kind he liked, high up and not too deep but wide, with small nipples that were almost lavender. Looking down, he could see her navel too above the thin, golden shorts, and her waist was surprisingly narrow for a woman who'd had a child. He put out his cupping palms to fondle her breasts—

"Let go of my mom!"

Press wrenched his head around sharply to stare at the redfaced ten-year-old standing in the doorway. Luke Simmons, mad as hell, his fists clenched with fury and his teeth gleaming in a snarl. The dentist's mouth fell open.

Luke hurtled toward the corner of his room snatching something in his hands, then whirled back, a baseball bat in his hands. It was a Louisville Slugger with Pete Rose's logo emblazoned on it, and the child had it raised above his head—he was *swinging* the meaty part of it, taking two steps toward the dentist. Without another word, Press Sumner ran, took off at top speed, the boy charging after him with the bat describing an arc.

Ginny blinked her eyes, conscious that someone was near, then peered innocently around. "Luke, honey?" she called. "Is that you?"

The headache that had been nagging in Cort Devalyn's head so long now that was beginning to feel it had become permanent got so bad, that August afternoon, that he came home early from Von Braun to take a nap. Ellie scarcely spoke to him as he passed her on his way to the bedroom, stripping off his shirt and sweated T-shirt, but that was all right. What he required now, he felt, was neither sex nor sympathy. Even immortality was meaningless at the moment, especially if it meant he'd have to endure this piercing throb in his temples and the cutting ache at the base of his head. He dropped onto the bed, pulling a clean sheet over him, groaning.

He was asleep the minute his painful head nestled into a pillow . . .

Impressions of something moving, crawling. How much time had passed, Cort didn't know. All he knew was that he was conscious, again, and someone—or *something*—seemed to be in bed with him.

Something that made him feel oddly . . . *creepy*. Frightened, if it came down to that.

At the windows, the curtains were drawn, the early evening was overcast, and he found it hard to make out the shadows lying like discarded wraps around the bedroom. Some of them looked *humped*, almost as though something lurked on the floor, waiting for him. Foolishness, he thought, childish foolishness. Without lifting his head, Cort blinked his eyes to clear his visions and stared harder at the pillow next to his, where Ellie generally lay.

His mouth grew dry. There *was* something there. The sheet was lifted well off the mattress, rounded as if it concealed a form of some kind. When he squinted to see it more clearly, Cort realized that the form was breathing. Steadily, rhythmically, the sheet rising and falling. And when he listened, he realized that it wasn't Ellie's breathing.

Because Ellie's breathing wasn't wheezing and raspy, tortured, as if the creature lying on the bed had some snoutish nose that did not allow normal, *human* breathing.

That was the point when he saw that the thing's hand was free of the sheet, and covered with stiff tufts of coal-black hair.

Cort cleared his throat.

Then words came not to Cort's ears but to his mind, searing his head.

I am he who guides the dead through the underworld to the kingdom of Osiris. I am the messenger who toils between heaven and hell. I am . . . the devourer.

"*Anubis?*" whispered Cort Devalyn, shrinking as far back

THE DENTIST

on his side of the bed as he could get. "You—*Anubis?*" He put out a hand to draw back the sheet.

See my face and die! the creature bellowed in Cort's brain, was a ramrod of acute pain that speared his mind, held it on a spit and roasted it over hellfire. *I come to warn you, son of Bellefontaine. It was your choice to seek out those who sleep, to disturb our rest. Now you must succeed or perish. Make the sacrifices of Tuat, to Meshkent—to Nekhebet and Hert-Ketit-S—as you arouse Thoth—and eternity shall belong to you and the nome. Take the life of he who is close and you shall have his years, multiplied a millionfold. Fail—and you are mine!*

For an instant the sheet slipped away and Cort Devalyn looked into the eyes of Anubis, jackal-headed god of the dead, he who was abandoned by Nephthys and reared by the goddess Isis; he who embalmed Osiris and invented the rites of the dead. The eyes of the immortal seared the teacher's soul, burned their image indelibly in his feverish mind; and then the bed was empty, the sheet collapsing to the mattress, as a stench like the foul fragrances of Hades' inner chamber left the teacher dizzied and choking.

When he could, Cort rose and put on his bathrobe. The wool felt rough on his naked arms and chest. Tottering, he moved into the hallway and glanced at his wristwatch. They had let him sleep through dinner; it was almost nine o'clock.

Cort paused outside Brian's bedroom. His eldest son was seated at his desk, doing his summer reading. Brian wasn't an advanced student; he wasn't a genius, like his little friend Luke. He didn't attend Von Braun High School, but crumbling old Stevenson High. And the tall man realized with a measure of surprise that he loved this child who had obliged him to get married at an embarrassingly early age, this boy-man who, until this very instant, had seemed so much Cort Devalyn's inferior.

"Brian?" he called softly.

The boy turned, startled. He dropped his pencil, then chuckled because it was silly to be scared by one's own father. "Hi, Dad. Y'feelin' any better?"

"Much, Brian, thank you." The teacher hesitated, then plunged, certain at last that he could not withdraw from his commitment. "I just wanted to remind you of that little surprise Uncle Press and I promised you."

Brian grinned. They'd told him of it a few days ago, a reward the two adult companions had planned, something nice because he was bringing his grades up now and wouldn't lose a year after all. Brian hoped it would be a new ten-speed. "I remember, Dad," he said lightly. "Saturday night at Uncle Press' office, right?"

Cort pointed at his son, made a little popping sound as if his finger had gone off. "On the nose!" He smiled broadly, paternally, then remembered to add something. "It's just the three of us, Brian, okay? Our secret!"

Brian made the point-and-popping right back. "Gotcha!"

In the other room, in her little alcove where she did astrology, Ellie heard them without having to listen hard. She looked down at the horoscope of her firstborn, progressed to Saturday night. Both Saturn and Uranus afflicted his sun sign.

Ellie's heartbeat began to accelerate. She had to do something. But what?

SEVENTEEN

Saturday night. Whenever either Press Sumner or Cort Devalyn thought those two words, they seemed to glow in quivering neon in their minds. And at the thirty-six-hour mark—a day and a half away from their carefully planned assault on mortality—the anthropologist had the dentist on the telephone, whispering to him about avoiding last-minute mistakes, exhorting him to make sure that the office was prepared.

"You almost ruined everything with that idiotic pass you made at Ginny Simmons," Cort told him, "and I'm not quite sure yet how you got by with it. Except she isn't clear about what happened, and the child hasn't said a word to either of his parents."

"It must be some sort of hypnotic lag, a valley of breakdown in Virginia's mind and then a new peak," Press said, not without gratitude to those gods whose favor they sought. "I've told you a thousand times I'm sorry. I won't let anything like that happen again."

"There's something more you can do to guarantee our success," the teacher continued. "My entire concept is based upon finding the pathway through preliminary, subsequent, and culminating sacrifices. But the pain we've inflicted together has been the key."

"What do you want me to do?" Press asked, already afraid to know.

"I want you to spread pain to everybody who sits in your chair on Friday," Cort commanded. "It doesn't matter even if they've only come to have their teeth cleaned. Hell, Press, what Alan said once is true. Everybody expects a dentist to deliver pain. Psychologically, they're practically disappointed if it doesn't hurt."

Press paused. "You're right. In the past, when everything's gone smoothly and I told the patient it was over, they looked at me like I hadn't done it right. As if I'd only poked around in their mouth and hadn't done enough for my fee." He sighed. "Okay, I'll do it. By the time I'm done today there won't be a house in town without someone in terrible pain."

He was as good as his word. Gritting his own teeth in fierce, single-minded determination, beginning with the first patient of the day—an attractive woman in her forties named Harriet McDuff—and working through an old man named Gerald Wilinson, Doctor Preston Sumner lived up to that secret, unspoken reputation which every dentist is afraid he might have. Pangs of torment ripped through gums. Agony

THE DENTIST

leaped from incisors. Blood gushed from around molars and flowed in the dentist's spit-fountain until it could scarcely be washed away. Closed wounds became draining, open wounds—wisdom teeth were mauled, torn out at awkward angles that left nerves singing like a chorus of the damned. Nightmare grief lived in the daytime, in Stevenson; mumbled curses and imprecations and lurching screams reverberated in the corners of Press Sumner's offices like writhing things that would never go away.

By the time it was five-oh-five in the afternoon and his last patient was reeling out the door, Press' suite was totally prepared for the culminating rites of immortality. Terrible pain batted against the ceiling like blinded bats or birds; the haunting of the place was complete.

He telephoned Cort from his back office, staring at his own bloodied whites with repugnance. They discussed it for a moment and then the anthropologist congratulated him, told him what a good job he'd done. Trembling, Press sighed.

"Tomorrow night," he began, concerned that his senior partner not err, but halfway hoping that the sometimes arrogant Devalyn had shown a human streak, "how do you plan on getting the brat to my office?"

"Leave that to me. The child appears to be naturally intuitive and I intend to use it against him." The teacher paused, reflecting. "He's really such an extraordinary child that it's a pity what must be done with him. It would be intellectually intriguing to learn if all people born with teeth in their mouths have a higher IQ than average. Certain tests indicate—"

"How?" the dentist pressed, although he was eager to

change clothes, to wash away the smell of blood clinging to him. "How will you get him here?"

"It's simple," Cort said into the phone. "Luke doesn't know that I know, but he's been spying on me. Regularly, from down the street. He's used binoculars." Cort laughed wryly. "Really, it's rather amusing the way he is the only one to catch on—the one who's never doubted for weeks that we were up to something. When he comes to spy on me tomorrow, Press, I will simply allow him to follow me to your office. He's much too small to make any kind of effective scene, or escape."

When the conversation was done, Cort Devalyn hung up and sat for a long moment by himself. He heard Ellie preparing dinner in the kitchen. The realization that Press had made his office physically suitable to their experiment gave Cort an enormous appetite for food and then, he thought with an ardor that was almost dreamy, with arousal he'd never experienced before this week, for sex. A pity little Press could not understand how similar women actually were and felt that he had to sample all their delicacies. Common sense said that this would prove impossible for Press, of course, regardless of how effective Saturday night was. There were limits to any man's endurance.

But for himself, for a Cort Devalyn who was only beginning to realize how inordinately special he was, there was no problem at all. For the practical and realistic man, who understood that the quality of the climax was all that mattered, one woman was plenty. People spoke these days of how liberated women had become, how they were freed to make their own choices; but the truth was that he could enjoy sex with Ellie until she died and there really wasn't a thing she

The Dentist

could do about it. Cort chuckled softly. The male remained exclusively in charge of the relationship so long as he kept her loving him. Why, Ellie would put up with anything at all, really, if he remembered to stroke her childish hand occasionally and whispered absurdities about love, the obligation she had to him, and the glorious things they'd do together someday. Recently, perhaps, he'd neglected some of the finer points, but tonight he'd be tender, he'd play on her sympathies, make a few pledges, and all would be well again.

Cort stretched his long legs, relaxed about their prospects now. Nothing could go wrong when you planned with perfection. And it was nice to allow oneself a moment of nostalgia, to recall how the whole thing began.

His approach had been wrong at the start, he knew now, because he'd looked at the question from an entirely scientific viewpoint. He'd spent too long, a year ago, evaluating what other men of genius had to say when he should have trusted his own instincts.

Instead, he'd considered the fact that there were strong evolutionary arguments against the achievement of immortality. The ecosystem of the planet earth was dynamic, perpetually in change, and it wouldn't permit a large portion of its biomass to be separated from the general life-flow. Natural evolution sought to adapt a species to its own earthly environment by means of a distinctly variable gene pool, and didn't allow individuals much leeway in adapting themselves significantly. If it was done in a rigid scientific fashion, an approach to genuine immortality tended to doom the species to stagnation. That path led to extinction.

Not that any of that mattered much to Cort, who was anxious only for personal immortality. Oh, it would have been nice to endow Ellie and the kids with the gift; but even then, a year ago, he'd sensed that any discovery he made would be unacceptable to them. And the facts made it obvious to him that his method would have to be unscientific.

In a way, life was already immortal, some experts said. Our bodies all carry ancient genetic materials so that each of us represents the entire species. Viewed in this somewhat generous way, man had always been man, and each of us was fundamentally the same physical organism, in loose terms— the same collection of basic genetic qualities—which existed at the time man first trod the earth. We were merely more richly adapted to this moment in time, specialized enough to reflect the additional evolutionary advancements since half-a-million years ago. Then there was also the old-fashioned attitude that, by procreating, a man and woman exercised a kind of immortality. Well, Cort chuckled scornfully, thinking of how unlike him Brian was—how rambunctiously full of enervating life the younger children were—that was just idiotic! He might *love* Brian, but Brian wouldn't be like Cort Devalyn if he lived to be a thousand. And the one thing Cort was sure of, tonight, was that love didn't interest him much any more.

Cloning, now—getting a person *exactly* like oneself—had possibilities. He saw one of Ellie's cigarette packs nearby and picked it up. One was left. When a man was meant to live forever, what fear should he have of the various cancers? He lit up, coughing some, and leaned luxuriously back to pick up the thread of his memories. There were modern experts in the field of longevity who believed (Cort knew) that a species' gene pool could never completely get rid of fatal cell-failure coding, that any concerted effort to make life meaningfully

THE DENTIST

longer necessitated selecting for reproduction later rather than earlier. Nature often protected the human being through the childbearing years, so that he might continue the race. But if the species were altered, if people did not naturally mate until age eighty or ninety, say—or one hundred and twenty; or two hundred—certain immunities might be in effect until the later-childbearing race had its chance to reproduce!

When Cort had summed up this information plus a great deal more last year, he'd seen that genetic engineering for immortality seemed a long-range answer to old age's infirmities and something that was likely to succeed eventually—but not until one Cort Devalyn, anthropology teacher and genius, was at least a very old man. And spending five-hundred to a thousand years in the body of a crippled or dessicated human being was not what he'd ever had in mind.

Odd the way he'd had his breakthrough. He glanced idly through the door to the kitchen, saw Ellie industriously at work and made a promise to himself to congratulate her cooking and massage her ego. Strange, but it wasn't till he began having his recurrent headaches—and began learning from his own subconscious mind more about his childhood and the man who had conceived him—that the germ of Cort's grand plan swam in the sea of his fertile brain.

But once he'd obtained the priceless, missing documents of ancient Egypt, he was well on his way to success. The separated information missing from the papyrus of Ebers finally suggested to Cort how it had been done, thousands of years ago—how the pharaohs were interred in their pyramids *only after they'd already survived hundreds of years of life—* and the fact that he'd had no slaves with which to generate

213

intense pain and open the pathway to eternity hadn't slowed the anthropologist for more than a minute.

With the little dentist's help, he'd merely created his *own* slaves.

Press Sumner among them, in a manner of speaking.

Cort had found it necessary to lie to the man to get his cooperation, to tell the fellow that a single talisman would be enough for both of them. It wouldn't be, of course. Cort had had to play on the dentist's desperate hunger for friendship, for acceptance; he'd been obliged to let Press think he liked him, trusted his judgment, valued him as a companion. The truth was, Cort thought he was disgusting.

Press Sumner had already had all he was ever going to get for his efforts, his sacrifices, his single-minded investment in the dealing of pain and misery. Oh, there might yet be an enhancement of the sex appeal and charm which their early efforts had brought the oral surgeon, but that would prove ultimately temporary, at best. A lot of his success had already sprung from the way that he *believed* he was more likeable, more desirable; and when he found himself again beginning to age—when the instant came that he knew he was old, and doomed to die—Press would realize that the only immortal left was his old friend, Cort Devalyn.

Yes, Cort mused, pleased with himself, I'm my father's son. I'm more like Georges Bellefontaine every day. But I'll succeed where he, with all his genius and cruelty, never came close.

"Dinner's ready, everybody," Ellie called in her chirping, affectionate voice.

It was almost startling, the normality of his wife's message, and there was a moment when elements of the Cort Devalyn whom Ellie married struggled to emerge.

Then Cort Bellefontaine readied his most ingratiating smile as he unfolded his tall, lanky body and headed languidly toward the dining room. *And so am I, my sweet*, he thought, already feeling the heat in his loins. *And so am I.*

EIGHTEEN

Although he'd been badly frightened twice by witnessing things he could not fathom, little Luke Simmons had soon rallied and begun returning to his observation point outside Cort and Ellie Devalyn's apartment. Once he'd heard the chubby blonde woman scream in apparent pain, and he'd seriously considered charging into the place in an effort to save her from whatever the tall teacher was doing. But his own mother hadn't seen fit to mention to anybody how he'd saved *her*, so heroically, from the ugly little dentist. Adults were funny people. It was impossible to know how Aunt Ellie would react, and if she wasn't grateful for his appearance, former Uncle Cort would be quite a handful.

He was fully unaware that his mother had no conscious recollection that Preston Sumner had tried hypnotically to rape her.

At first, it had required courage to go back to the Devalyn apartment and spy. Luke felt that there were things going on there that were quite beyond the scope of himself or his parents. While he genuinely believed that he himself was better equipped intellectually than either Alan or Ginny to handle most problems of any importance, Luke knew he was no match for a grown adult. Cort made two of him.

But there'd been no overt threats of any kind against him and he was sure that nobody knew he was outside watching. Besides, there is scarcely a boy anywhere—genius or otherwise—who doesn't succumb at one time or another to the notion of playing detective. And so eventually Luke had not only returned to his post but had begun taking Lucy Sumner with him, consciously for "disguise" and unconsciously for company.

He couldn't be there all the time, of course. He was stuck in summer school for two hours each day. But there'd been ample time in the afternoons and early evenings to keep tabs on the anthropology teacher's comings and goings, and Luke had started compiling a dossier, of sorts, a record which he kept in the back of an old notebook. Twice, he'd actually followed the lanky instructor—once with Lucy tightly gripping his hand, ducking with him into the shadows—all the way to Von Braun High. He regarded it as important that Cort sometimes let himself into the school after it was closed.

Thus, by the time Saturday rolled around, Luke had been lulled into a false sense of security—one that might easily have trapped far older persons than he.

It was the Simmons' family custom to sleep late on Saturdays, whenever it was possible, and nobody awakened until nearly eleven o'clock. Luke arose quietly, took care of his morning ablutions, then returned to awaken Lucy. A few whispered words were exchanged and he learned that she wanted to go with him that afternoon on the spying mission. Luke rather imagined that the little girl simply enjoyed getting out for a walk, but that was okay. He enjoyed her company. "I'll come back later to get you," he said, surprised when she dropped promptly back into sleep.

Alan, his father, surprised him further by being present in his own front room chair, waiting for the boy. One look at the way Dad was tapping his fingernails on the arm of the chair was enough to notify Luke that last night's chewing out—for being late for dinner—wasn't over.

But seeing Dad with his belt lying threateningly across his lap was a new feature, and the boy's eyes widened. Never before had his father given him worse than a spanking.

"I want to know where in hell you've been going lately," Alan said between tightly clenched teeth.

"The usual places, I guess," Luke answered as casually as possible. He tried not to look at the belt. "I'm sorry I was late last night." He paused, then decided to add a reminder. "I told you that then."

"Don't get sassy with me, young man!" Alan warned him. "You know, I think you've been getting more and more high and mighty ever since you found out your IQ. Well, let me tell you that intelligence isn't worth a damn when it's not used."

"That's true," Luke admitted, but it sounded impertinent.

"Do you think it's smart to make your mother and father worry about you?"

"Dad," the boy said quickly, wide-eyed and reasonable, "I'm perfectly capable of looking out for myself. Really I am. You don't have to worry about me."

Alan was steaming now. "Which means, if I interpret young Professor Simmons' meaning correctly—in the lowly abyss of my own meager intellect—that if we worry about you, that's basically *our* problem. Correct?"

Luke covered one tennis shoe toe with another, shying away from a direct reply. He chose a different tack and, in doing so, displayed particularly bad judgment. "Dad, I wish you wouldn't be jealous because my IQ is higher. It's not your fault at all that yours isn't as high as mine. I was just lucky."

Alan Simmons saw red. He was on his feet now, unable to keep from lashing out once with the belt. It wrapped around Luke's small buttocks stingingly with a crackling sound that startled them both. Feeling badly about striking his only son in such a way for the first time, the father compounded his guilt. "I should have known when you were born that I'd have trouble, that you were different than other people!" He was perspiring, breathing hard, his angry face feet from the boy's. "Sometimes I think we gave birth to a goddam *Martian* instead of a child like anybody else's!"

Luke hand rose to his mouth in shock. "It's my darned old teeth," he realized, staring in deep injury at his father. "You think I'm a weirdo because I was born with teeth!"

"Well, I believe they made us treat you differently," Alan retorted, backing down a little. The hurt expression on his son's face was ringing warning bells in his customarily clear mind. "They made us treat you like you were—really special—

when we should have handled you like we would any other small child."

The harm was done. Luke ran to the door of the apartment, fighting back tears. "You never liked me!" he shouted. "I guess I knew that all along. You *always* thought I was a damned *freak*, right, Dad?"

"I didn't say that," Alan called. He stood frozen to the spot in front of the chair, horrified by what he had said. The belt fell unnoticed from his open hand to the floor. Anger, heightened by the strange things going on around him, had now oozed away. "I never said we didn't want you, son, and I never said you were a freak."

"But you thought it!" Luke tore the door open. Now the tears began to flow despite his efforts to restrain them, contorting his expression. "Well, maybe I can s-still make you proud of me if I find out what's h-happening in town! Maybe I can show you I'm a little more than just a f-freak!"

Then he was outside, dashing down the steps into a shocking spray of sunshine, unsure where he was going but glad to be away.

For several hours Luke roamed the busy Saturday streets of Stevenson, cutting dangerously between cars full of shoppers and twice going past the Devalyn apartment building. There he found the shades drawn, the rooms dark. Presumably the Devalyns slept late the way the Simmonses did. Trying not to think of his problems at home, Luke lost track of the time, wasn't even aware where he was headed or even where he happened to be at a given moment, and he didn't care. His tears finally dried up but the pang of wounded feelings hadn't left. Nor had his determined desire to atone, somehow, for being born different.

It seemed to Luke that he'd always been oddly apart from his parents, his grandparents, their neighbors, his own friends. Not a lot, maybe—nobody treated him really *bad*, except that bully Ronnie Baker—but enough to let him know he was the one thing no young person anywhere wants to be; different. For such people, if they are fortunate, there comes a time when they wish to perform some act that makes the troublesome problem of difference worthwhile, that validates essential worth. He'd reached that point by a few minutes before five o'clock in the evening, when he headed quietly homeward.

Luke slipped into the apartment unseen. Lucy was waiting, clad in a one-piece checkered playsuit but barefoot. She was delighted he'd remembered to come back for her. Luke put her shoes on, and tied the strings. He could hear his mother in the kitchen, humming a Rodgers and Hammerstein song.

Helping her to her feet, Luke took the girl by the hand and went out to the front room where an unpleasant feeling washed over him. It was unformed, unclear; it might have been a premonition of danger, but he chalked it up instead to imagination. He left a note he'd written where he'd planned to leave it, for Dad. Then he retrieved his binoculars from the closet. Together, he and the smaller child hurried out to the sidewalk without seeing a soul.

The streets glared with late-afternoon light and the humidity made things look almost foggy. There was, Luke thought, an uncanny timelessness in the air as well, almost as if the town held its collective breath, waiting for something. He was glad when the two of them reached the Devalyn apartment building.

Moments later, the tall anthropology teacher himself emerged, alone, from the front door of the brick building,

THE DENTIST

catching the small boy offguard. He drew Lucy back into the shadows of a convenient jewelry store, which had been boarded up since before Luke began his spying career. Cort did not look in their direction at all but began walking west, to Luke's additional surprise. Von Braun High, where Luke had supposed the adult meant to go, lay east of the apartment building.

Gripping Lucy's hand tightly, to make sure she didn't dash into the street, he set off after Cort, keeping a steady block behind the adult, deeply curious about Devalyn's destiny. He took such long, purposeful strides that it was hard for Lucy to keep up, until she began to trot along, humming a tune as she went.

He observed that Cort Devalyn looked to have lost considerable weight from his already slender body, although that hardly seemed possible in one day. Cort wore his usual sports jacket and walking shorts and the legs protruding in pale haste seemed scarcely adequate to support his weight. Indeed, the quick figure looked emaciated as it began stepping now into the newly falling shadows.

Suddenly Cort stopped. Without looking back, he was fumbling for something in his jacket pocket. Something that looked to Luke, as it rested in the teacher's palm, like a gray mouse. Then the man appeared to be satisfied, slipped it back into his pocket and continued to walk. Luke saw now where they were heading: the one-story structure that housed the dental offices of Doctor Preston Sumner.

The boy's heartbeat quickened; it fairly boomed in his chest. The building crouched like a pasty lizard a considerable distance back from the street in a little trafficked neighborhood, its front porch a flicking tongue. Not a single car passed. The one-story structure was pinned between several aging, gaunt trees that made it appear huddled in waiting. While the house had been painted white that spring, the tenants—Press Sumner and a self-employed realtor, who was rarely present—seldom saw to it that the front lawn was mowed. Grass and weeds had sprung up a foot, in concealing clumps. The scene had an ambience not so much of abandonment but of cold neglect, as if the house had other things on its mind. To Luke, half a block away, grasping Lucy's hand, there was something oddly animal-stealthy about the way the sun's dying rays glinted on the building, beneath the front gutter. The two windows appeared to be winking hooded eyes at him, squinting warily from around a pair of stark, ebon elms.

All along, Luke had felt that these two adults—Doc Sumner; Cort Devalyn—were in this together, whatever "this" turned out to be. He hadn't liked the way Cort had been lurking in the dentist's surgery when no one but Press knew he was inside, and he hadn't cared for the way Devalyn spoke praisingly of pain. He still wondered what Press had been doing, exactly, to his parents and he remembered vividly how they had seemed drugged, disoriented. He hadn't thought the homely oral surgeon's attmpted attack on his mother was totally unrelated, either, although he couldn't imagine in what manner it was connected. To Luke, the presence of something secret was clear as the sunlight reflecting off the dentist's windowglass.

The dentist's building was going to be hard to spy on. Luke began laying plans. There were plenty of trees for two small people to hide behind. He decided that he and Lucy would stay well back from the front door but, when Cort Devalyn

THE DENTIST

was inside, they would try to see through the window. He smiled secretly. If what was happening turned out to be bad enough, and Luke fetched his father in time to see it, too, Dad just might be glad he'd had a newborn with teeth, one who was freakishly smart. He might not only atone for his peculiarities but wind-up covered with glory.

Ahead of them something fell from the tall teacher's pocket. Devalyn didn't seem to notice it. No, he was going right on inside, closing the door behind him. And the object—that precious item he'd been checking, only moments ago—lay by itself on the porch.

It's the talisman! the boy realized with excitement. *He's dropped his secret talisman!*

There are memorable moments in any young boy's life when curiosity has a way of throttling common sense, however brilliant the boy may be. Those adventures that he will only see in movies, when he reaches adulthood, somehow appear only passingly hazardous at the age of ten. Boys scarcely know what death is; they believe nothing bad can happen to them, and they haven't yet learned how terrible the human species can be.

Motioning to Lucy to follow him, Luke stooped low and made a swift beeline for the porch of the building. The children landed softly on it, without a single creaking noise their eyes huge and their hearts racing. Luke took *one, two, three* tiptoeing steps toward the fallen talisman, stooped to pick it up—

And heard the heavy footsteps behind him and the girl. He spun to face them.

Cort Devalyn stood on the top step, blocking their path to the street. Shadows pressed in around his elongated body.

"Let us go," Luke said in a husky voice, raising the pouch to eye level. "I've got your talisman, and I'll destroy it if you don't let us leave."

"You're a very intelligent boy, Luke," the teacher said admiringly. "But not, I fear, as bright as you think. Go ahead. Empty the pouch. I really don't care."

Luke paused, frowning up at the adult. Then he did precisely that. There was a grayish swirl in the air like chunky motes of dust, and the bag was empty. Luke tossed it at the tall man's feet and then looked defiantly up at him.

Cort smiled. His long fingers parted his sports shirt at the neck. They dipped, raised a cord. And hanging from the cord was a pouch of expensive leater.

The door opened behind Luke and Lucy.

Doctor Preston Sumner stood in the doorway, his mane of hair gleaming, his teeth shining in grotesque mimicry of a welcoming smile. "I think you'd better come inside," he said.

NINETEEN

By the time eight-thirty came and there'd been no sign of either Luke or Lucy Sumner, Ginny was frantic with worry.

It seemed unthinkable to her that her son would miss dinner for a second night in a row. Luke wasn't usually that calloused, or that forgetful—especially since she and Alan had given him such a good talking to Friday evening. He would have been terrified to disobey them two nights running, particularly since he'd taken Lucy with him. Without mentioning it to Alan, she went to the phone in the dining room to call her friend Ellie Devalyn. Maybe Ellie had seen him.

Alan's mind was a turmoil of anxiety and confused emotions. On the one hand, there was the fact that he couldn't forget how he'd hurt Luke, how the boy had looked when he left the apartment late that morning. His little face had been a thundercloud behind the thick-lensed glasses. On the other hand, there was the fact that he'd taken Lucy along, apparently teaching the little girl how to disobey and putting Alan in one hell of a spot if Press Sumner happened to stop by. What in the name of God could he tell the dentist—that he just didn't know where his precious daughter was?

Alan had intended to make it up to the kid until Luke failed to show up for dinner. He had planned to take both the kids to the Indians' closing baseball games of the season, before the parent Red called up half the team. Or maybe, if he could manage to swing it, he'd buy them season tickets for the Indiana Pacers' games—tickets just for Luke and him. The boy was forever dunking paperwads in the wastebaskets as he pretended to be a star.

As the dinner hour came and went, however, Alan was in a different mood. A man's mood. He hated it when anything interfered with his major meal of the day. Ginny often told their friends that if a president were assassinated at dinnertime Dan Rather would have to wait until later to make the announcement—or maybe Alan would just catch it on Nightline.

When he'd been obliged to poke his food around on the plate for half an hour, finding it tasteless, Alan stopped thinking Luke was "hurt somewhere," as he had for the last fifteen minutes. Before that he'd spent a quarter-hour believing that Luke had taken Lucy and run away. Now Alan concluded that the boy was simply trying to establish that he could do anything he wished and get by with it.

Thus it was that when Ginny phoned Ellie, at eight-thirty, Alan was furiously dumping himself into his easy chair in the front room, determined to restore his own routine (and dignity) by reading the evening *News*.

Moments later he'd run to the dining alcove to stand by Ginny, at the phone, gesturing to her to hang up.

When she saw the wrinkled, grubby note in his hand, she did.

"He put this where he figured I'd find it," Alan said, his voice so tight it was trembling. "Between the book pages of the Free Time section of the paper."

Ginny snatched it away from him. "What does it say?" she asked.

"The only thing I really understand," Alan replied, watching her anxious eyes scan the page of Luke's large-lettered handwriting, "is that we aren't supposed to worry." He swallowed hard.

"*Dear Mom and Dad,*" Ginny read, aloud, "*I've always let you both down by being bad-different, so now it's time to make you proud of me by getting good-different. Lucy is safe with me. We're both fine, I promise. If we make it, we'll have big news soon. Don't worry and back real soon. Love, Luke S. (And Lucy too)*"

Ginny read it all a second time, looking for more clues. Then she lowered the crumpled paper, raising her gaze to Alan. Tears were forming deep in her green eyes like water rising from the bottom of a pool. Neither knew what to say. What was worse, neither of them knew what to do.

"The people of the world have always gone to great pains to prepare for the trip to the other side. You should all be thrilled, if you had the proper historical sense, that we are going to such great pains for you. It was kings and pharaohs, primarily, who received the kind of attention Doctor Sumner and I have planned."

It was hot in Preston Sumner's office with all the windows closed and locked and the air conditioner running low. They had placed black and white candles so that they circled the surgery completely, forming an unbroken line, now that they were all in the center. In addition, small statuettes Cort had collected, which had once been used in Egyptian rites of death, rung the circle. Called *Ushabti*, made of wood and faience, they were inscribed with prayers taken from the *Book of the Dead* and were carved in the shape of watchful, anthropomorphic cobras. It was getting dark outside, and fantastic shadows rose from the candles that were already lit.

Cort felt brilliant, he marveled at how easy it was being. He sensed the right kind of excitement, the variety that made the adrenaline flow, cleared the brain of absurd personal considerations, and enabled one to be at his bright and fluent best. His keen eyes scanned the unwilling group Press and he had assembled in the surgery, deeply pleased.

Cort's own son Brian had been on time, full of smiling expectations. He'd been given the same mild sedative administered by Press to the others: enough to keep each of them physically relaxed, almost to the point of inability to move, but not so much that it kept them from alert thinking. The last thing in the world the dentist wanted to do was stymie their natural ability to feel pain.

Now Brian and Lucy Sumner were trussed up in sitting positions. Luke—whose newborn teeth had started it all— had been placed in the seat of honor: Press' dental chair. As Cort addressed them, in his finest teaching manner, Press stood behind his little girl, stroking her red hair and looking half-drugged. In point of fact, he was; it had been his own idea. Full of Valium, he would not muster an objection when the time came to destroy his child.

"Even Cro-Magnon man was thoughtful in disposing of his own kind," Cort was saying, his inflections rich, "and prehistoric man fifty thousand years ago left his dead brother with a smattering of food and tools. The Etruscans, young Luke—whom you claim to have studied—have been found to place in the tombs of the dead *living horses* in readiness for the finest chariots."

Luke worked hard to make his mouth work against the drug. "I—know that."

"And I believe you," Cort said in simple praise, an angry gaze flicking at his own son, Brian. "But did you know that it was the Egyptians, more than any other ancient race, who had the intelligence to see that a lifetime was short, a *deadtime* long—and knew what to do about it?" The teacher's eyes widened, flamed. "It wasn't understood until I came along that the mummies of Egypt's greatest pharaohs contained bodies that were already hundreds of years old when wrapped. You see, Luke, they knew that for the soul of *ka* to survive, it was necessary for the body to survive as well." Now he beamed on Luke. "It took your Uncle Cort to discover why only *some* pharaohs had pyramids built in their honor, and what they do! They were constructed only for brilliant rulers who'd already lived for centuries. Today there are those who perceive that a unique power emits from the pyramidal structure—but its full effects can only be experienced by the pharaohs who lived two or three hundred years before they died. In the year 2000, my brilliant student, all those ancient rulers will again sit up, will stand and walk, ready for yet another two or three hundred years of actual life!"

"Can I—ask you—a question?" Luke mumbled, turning his head from side to side, combating the drug.

"Certainly, my boy!"

"Why d'you—wear—those ridiculous shorts? You look—silly in them!"

Cort gaped in fury at the helpless boy. In a moment, however, his shoulders were shaking in silent amusement. "I understand, Luke. This is your valiant way of dealing with a difficult situation. I respect that, really I do." He looked at Lucy, who was close to sleep and had no idea what was happening, at his son Brian, and back to Luke Simmons. "Do all of you want to know what is going on this night? Would you like an understanding, not only of what is to be done with you but what your sacrifices will create?"

For an instant there was no answer. Then Brian Devalyn, who'd seen a lot of movies in his fourteen years, cleared his throat to offer a response. "I'd like to know, Dad. If we really—must die for something—I'd like—to know what it is." *Stall, Brian* he told himself firmly. *Stall.*

"Very well, son. I suppose it's better that you begin asking intelligent questions now than never in your young life." Cort hesitated, gathering his wily thoughts, gloriously free of his headache for the first time in months. He began pacing, hands behind his back. He might have looked no more frightening than a man chasing butterflies except for the peculiar intense flash in his eyes. "There is a first step that involves the three of you directly and, I fear, considerable pain. But allow me to return to that."

THE DENTIST

"When your sacrifice has been made, you will be placed in canopic jars." He glanced at Press, who nodded. "They already await you in the private office of your good Uncle Press."

"*Daddy*," Lucy Sumner murmured the correction, her eyes half-open now. A fragile smile visited her sweet lips simply because she liked the sound of the word. "*My daddy.*"

Cort felt the dentist's gaze burning his own and looked to the other children. "Canopic jars were, in ancient Egypt, containers for the dead until time of mummification began. Each is decorated with the heads of the Four Sons of Horus: Mesthi, representing the liver; Duamutef, guardian of the stomach; dog-headed Hapi, signifying the lungs; and Qebhsennuf, the hawk-headed representative of the intestines. Symbolically, children," the teacher continued, still pacing, "you will also be protected in your noble death by four goddesses: Isis, Neith, Neophthys and Serket."

"My God, Dad," Brian blurted out, jarred to something like full consciousness. "Do you mean to—turn us into *mummies?*"

"Alas, no," Cort said cheerily. "That knowledge is only now being restored and the art is used exclusively for pharaohs. Leaders. No, my boy, when your time of waiting in the canopic jars has passed—and all official inquiries, with it— you will enjoy a different fate." He lifted a scholarly index finger. "But it, too, is an honor no modern human being has experienced."

"What—honor?" Luke asked.

It was dark now, and one of the candles Preston Sumner had been quietly lighting illuminated the oddly benign countenance of Cort Devalyn—except that he was unquestionably

Cort Bellefontaine now, the outer layers of the civilized Devalyns finally stripped away to reveal the monstrous son of a monstrous father. "Why, the honor of being interred beneath the pyramidal structure called a mastaba," he said, "very, very deep in a pit filled with wet sand." The ghastly smile widened. "Only the greatest gods shall find you there."

For a timeless instant there was no sound. There was only the desperate staring of innocent children, who finally realized that their lives were in the hands of two madmen.

"You mentioned—a first step," Brian said. His heart was thumping furiously but he was continuing to stall, trying with an intelligence he'd never adequately used to find a means of escape. "One that involved—considerable pain."

"I'll allow Doctor Sumner to explain that," Cort remarked.

Press looked up from the candle he was lighting, his round face and blunt features turned yellow, the hollows of his cheeks the burnt umber of something that had died. He seemed surprised, at first; but then he collected his thoughts, looking exclusively at the boys, Luke and Brian. It was clear that he did not dare look at his sleeping daughter.

"We have reached our point of success," the dentist began, "by virtue of inflicting pain and opening the pathway to eternity. Our final steps must be taken on the same path, in the same way." He stuck a cigar in his mouth and let it jut out from there, unlit. His hard brown eyes rolled from face to face. "I shall be candid about it, say it straightforwardly to you, kids: We need all your teeth. Now." He saw their heads jerk in hideous understanding, and his cigar wobbled to the other corner of his mouth. "Yes, every tooth in your heads—

THE DENTIST

pulled in the most painful ways I can devise, in order to keep the pathway to immortality open and wide."

Brian's mouth fell open in shock. Luke shut his, tight, his lips protectively sucked in. The eyes of both boys were enormous with fright.

"Your teeth will then be pulverized, added to those in the precious talisman which Cort Devalyn wears for us both"—he saw the anthropology teacher incline his head slightly, smiling— "and when the *other* things he described are done, why, we will practically have achieved our goals." Press lifted the cigar from his mouth now, openly smiling. He passed his fingers through his dark mane of hair, then wiped them on his medical whites. His expression revealed the man. "Each of us will become beloved by all those who meet us, male and female. Each of us will therefore become more successful than we've ever dreamed. And each of us," he lit the cigar then, great clouds of foul-smelling smoke rising to the ceiling of his surgery, "will live forever."

TWENTY

Ellie hung up her phone and sat staring. For a moment she thought she saw the devil, suspended across the room in the gathering nightshadows, his smile intimate and leering.

But it was only the power of suggestion from talking with Ginny. It was Cort's face, instead, affixed in her subconscious mind; and she knew without a doubt why she had summoned his visage.

Her glance went to the silent phone again. She was hearing in her memory's ear Ginny Simmons' fright over the missing children. Cort, Ellie thought dully. He had them both. She knew that as certainly as she knew that he also had her own son Brian. She knew it because she remembered the lanky teacher's talk of necessary sacrifice, and she knew it because her maternal heart ached now as once her womb had ached.

Then, however, she was gaining life. This awful Saturday night she might be losing it.

But every woman, every man, pays first homage in the twentieth century to the gods of logic who are assembled in cool judgment within the brain—austere and stern, cynical entities who sit within in miniature straightback chairs around a conference table, tapping tiny fingers and tut-tutting at every flight of fancy. Even at every scrap of untraceable internal knowing. Ellie approached the gods now, appealed to them, and heard the litany that Cort and Press were both *fathers*, after all. The judges of rationalism insisted—because they were *her* judges, in *her* kind mind—that parents never harmed their children, always cherished them.

But the conference table was faced with a split vote. *Tap-tap*, went other stiff and haughty fingers; *tut-tut*, other throats were cleared; those views were not necessarily logical either, given the day and age.

What *was* the truth, then? She could not wait all night for the decision to be reached. Perhaps she no longer had time to do anything about what was happening.

Urgently, Ellie hurried to her astrology alcove, and began rummaging quickly through her collection of horoscopes. Her hands had become leaden and clumsy; several charts fell on the floor. Alan Simmons' chart; her mother's; Ronald Reagen's and Burt Reynold's and Elizabeth Taylor's charts and that cute little butcher at Safeway—where were the right horoscopes?

Frantic, or close to it, Ellie raced through two separate

THE DENTIST

piles and had them before her, staring down at them in the hope she was wrong.

But she wasn't, not astrologically at least. Her son Brian and Ginny's son Luke were in terrible danger. Aspects forming in transit afflicted Brian's Eighth House, his segment of potential physical annihilation; Luke's progressed planets were on the cusp of the Seventh, in opposition, showing he'd become his own worst enemy. Ellie touched each chart as though her fingers might draw the danger out of them. *Either* boy could die, that very night—and both of them might.

She began to rise, then changed her mind and drew out Cort's own horoscope.

Ellie hadn't looked at it in a long while, because he paid small attention to her predictions or advice, and because, in recent weeks, she hadn't cared much what became of him.

What she saw there now, what she read in her own shaking hand using three different color inks in order to trace the complexities of the man—saw in the array of squared and triangulated and indescribable shorthand marks of the world's most ancient art—startled her. She hadn't expected *this*. It involved Neptune, planet of delusion; Uranus, planet of sweeping and electrical change; and the moon, governing emotions and mankind's oldest symbol of mystery.

To verify her own findings she located two trusted old books—one by W. T. Tucker, another by Charles E. O. Carter—and swiftly checked the aspects, her lips mumbling words as a woman of another old faith might say her beads.

Blue eyes great with fright, certain there was no longer any question about it, Ellie Devalyn threw the books aside to scramble for the front door of her apartment, a desperate fact forming in her mind.

J. N. Williamson

If there was any validity to astrology at all, Cort Devalyn had gone stark, staring mad.

"There is somewhat *more* to the first stage," the lean anthropologist said in a whisper, his head oscillating from one to another of their captives. For the first time a note of something other than wild confidence and manic optimism had crept into his voice. The note sounded on the chill precipice of respect, and fear. "The summoning of One who will assist us, he who comes from the deepest ends of that pathway which we seek tonight: Anubis!"

Press Sumner was completing the preparations. Lighting the rest of the candles, their colors alternating black-white-black-white like some lunatic chessboard, he chose every twelfth candle and began dripping tallow in the form of a pentagram. The design took shape in front of the children—Luke, dozing Lucy Sumner and Brian Devalyn—and equidistant between the working dentist and the lecturing teacher.

Luke, whose reading was not only advanced for his meager ten years but imaginative and catholic, understood at once what they were doing. "You're calling—a demon?" he asked, staring at the adults and pulling his feet as far back on the dental chair as he could.

Brian's lips parted in shock. "Please, Dad," he said, his fourteen-year-old voice ringing in his nervousness from tenor to baritone, the words halting in his semi-drugged state, "I know I'm not—everything you wanted—but I'm still—*your son.*"

A dark eyebrow rose in the hollowed, emaciated face of Cort Bellefontaine. "Precisely," he replied. A twitch began at one corner of his mouth as he tried to smile. "Your honor will be the one that was meant to be mine, decades ago. No one would do, for my sacrifice, but you, just as the little girl had to be Doctor Sumner's sacrifice." He put out a long, thin arm that seemed snake-like in the candlelit surgery and his fingers trembled against the boy's cheek. "Be brave, as I was, knowing that your terrible pain and eventual death were personal only in the sense that you were of the Bellefontaine line."

"But Dad," Brian tried again, tears starting in his eyes, "don't—don't you love me?"

For a moment the intense teacher was too busy watching Press Sumner to answer. The short, stocky man stooped to complete the steaming, waxen pentagram and its vital, interlocking internal design. Then Press nodded and Cort snatched up the one candle left unlit—his own—to raise it high over his head. When he smashed it in the center of the ancient pentagram, it would start them irreversibly on the course to immortality.

But he looked back to the lad, at last, his head cocked at a strangely watchful angle, his eyes glittering with banked fury and frustation. "It is your generation that fouls its wits with illicit narcotics, that steals from the very place it nested, and sobs pitifully when it is finally apprehended, 'You should have loved me better.' No one ever loved *me*, my son. It's your generation that recognizes educational failure as a bold gesture of independence, bastardization as a whimsical lark, the continuity of family and the marital rite as that which is more temporary and insubstantial then the broken, feathered wing of a hummingbird—but which, it its infantile need, cries, 'Love me because I *am*.' Well, Brian, my son, I have reached the heights of achievement without the pewling hand of parental adoration stretched out to help me! You should have learned, by now, what the balance of achievement means in this cruel world—for this price you pay tonight is not as dear as that others of your generation must one day meet!" Cort blinked his eyes to hold back hot tears, crammed his hands beneath his armpits to avoid the urge to touch his son a last time. "Soon, Bri, fathers in every region of this world will see what a sham your generation is with all its cooings of love and peace and friendship, and find their *own* magical pathway to the accomplishments denied us by your feeble, throw-away generation! Soon, that one gift which you have used to blackmail us with—your youth—will belong to those who demand it!"

Brian held his gaze bravely and gestured to the smaller boy tied to the chair beside him. "Luke," he said. "Isn't Luke what your generation—has sought?"

The teacher exploded in laughter, the candle above his head shimmering from the convulsive force. At his designated point across the pentagram, Press Sumner stared at the taller, thinner man with anxiety. Cort's affection was going out to young Brian! Did that put the final steps in jeopardy?

"Bri," Cort Bellefontaine said, when he could, "you have actually enlightened me at last! I compliment you, boy! You have reminded me that my generation is just as degraded, self-serving and hypocritical as your own!"

With that, he smashed the candle into the exact heart of the steaming pentagram.

And as the homely dentist crouched above Luke, sharply-gleaming tools poised by the boy's helpless mouth to coordinate with the appearance of mighty Anubis, something utterly hideous began assuming shape.

THE DENTIST

* * *

"I k-know where Luke and Lucy have been taken," Ellie said haltingly, the instant the front door of the Simmons apartment swung wide.

Ginny and Alan stood immobile for an instant, the natural human need to ask questions strong in them. Alan had just finished an hour of telephoning every acquaintance of Luke's whom he knew, and had become as desperate as Ginny.

For her part, Ginny had reached her customary state, in emergency conditions: glacially calm, perfectly controlled on the outside, and totally self-destructive within. She touched Ellie's arm, as if making physical contact with someone who cared might make everything all right. "Where are the children?" she asked in her artificially level, low voice.

Ellie hugged her and began to cry. "I think C-Cort took them, he and that monstrous dentist," she said. "For some kind of—of sacrifice."

"They must be at Press Sumner's office," Alan said simply. "Let's go." He took his wife's arm and rushed her out of the apartment, Ellie running to keep up.

The night was hot, the humidity soaring. When they reached the curb, Alan hesitated, mopping his forehead with his sleeve and uncertain whether to drive his own car or take Ellie's. Since hers was already running, he half-shoved the two women into the front seat, mumbled, "I'll drive," and dropped hastily behind the steering wheel.

The Oldsmobile peeled away from the curb, laying two ribbons of rubber steaming behind them. Alan narrowly missed a Volkswagon Rabbit, making a turn into the apartment complex, and then he was spinning the Devalyn Olds

243

in a tight turn of its own and heading straight for the dental offices.

"I should have known it would be them," he said, a muscle working in his right cheek. "It's my fault, the whole damned thing. Luke tried to tell us and I wouldn't really listen, I wouldn't follow up on anything and demand the answers." He turned his anxious face to Ginny. "We'll make it in time, won't we?"

She gave him an anxious tender smile. "Of course, we will," she promised.

But inwardly, she didn't know. She didn't know at all.

Court Bellefontaine gaped at the apparition as it straightened from a crouch. The all-important talisman of pulverized teeth fell from the Egyptologist's trembling fingers. He lifted his thin arm, pointing at It as the realization of awful duplicity swept through him. *"You,"* he cried, *"You aren't Anubis!"*

The thing did not answer. It was still uncertainly defined, its vast and muscled body a hulking contour of shadow.

"What *is* it?" Press Sumner questioned in a hiss from the other side of the entity.

There was enough of the beast taking hideous shape that Cort Bellefontaine could identify it. He didn't want to. He wanted to scream; he recognized the terror.

His lips wrung out the reply to the frightened dentist: "This is the brother of Osiris and Isis, the personification of perversity, drought, and danger." He pointed to the high, erect ears of the creature, its ugly fang-lined muzzle. "This is he who was the pattern for Satan, in the earliest morning of Christianity." He pointed to the bright red hair of the monster, razor-sharp as it lifted in fierce tufts that ran in a grotesque mane down the back of its head. "This is the Egyptian god of evil, darkness, and destruction—called Set."

The beast had formed now and its countenance full and feral on the anthropologist. Curving horns, cement-hard and glittering as if polished, rose from the center of its skull, almost meeting in pincer-like formation. Drool from its smiling muzzle puddled the floor and steam rose from the splash. Eyes that had seen eternity or perhaps devised it, madly prominent in sockets placed above the foam-flecked muzzle, fixed on Cort in an adamantine brilliance and ferocity. They were not faintly . . . human. *"Call me Set, mortals— the god of all-Sin!"*

Shaking, Press Sumner could see only the entity's back, the bristling red bush-strip of cruel hair, the shoulders broad as any three men's put together, the rippling sensual muscles of its back, buttocks and oak-like legs; and the corded, whipping tail that lashed in pent-up passion from side to side. From the base of the spine to beneath the ankles and above the clawed feet, the beast was covered with the feathers of some fantastic fowl, multi-hued and vivid to the point of queerly impossible beauty.

Alan, Ginny and Ellie Devalyn threw open the door to the surgery and stood frozen on the threshold.

The monster, Set, ignored the newcomers. It stretched out its long neck until the wolfen muzzle was within inches of Cort's face. "You dropping, you're no match for your father!" it rumbled, and the candle ring in which it stood vibrated and flickered. "He, at least, kept us amused before his soul disintegrated. You're nothing but a fool!"

"Wh-why are you here?" Cort whispered, a hand raised uselessly. "I was p-promised immortality by Anubis . . ."

"You were deceived by my *own* hypnosis, my *own* needs and desires!" exclaimed Set, his tail swinging, forcing short Press Sumner into the farthest point of the candled circle. "I only *used* your desires, your foolish urge for eternal life, to force you to summon me." Something like a chuckle tumbled into the dental surgery like thunder clouds and a stench of ultimate filth permeated the room. "Had you stopped with the talisman—with the teeth of the child and those whom you'd dared to bring to such hellish pain—you might at least have enjoyed *this* life! Instead, you have allowed me to come for you!"

"But w-what *do* you want of us?" Cort asked, standing his ground.

Press Sumner whimpered from behind Set.

Great Set wheeled upon him. "What I want is what I *always* want. *This* will show you whether you command me or not!"

A single inhumanly massive fist rose, and fell. It caught the dentist on top of his skull and drove his head *into* his throat and shoulders, organs rupturing and bone splintering. At the door to the room Ginny Simmons cried out in revulsion. The jaw of Press Sumner had disappeared from view, into his own body, the top of his head shattering as scraps of gray brain splattered the floor.

Then the god turned back to Cort Bellefontaine Devalyn, the crimson hair behind its forehead standing erect with desire, its muzzle open hungrily, its tail twitching.

At that moment Alan ran as he had never run before, hurtling himself across the floor and into the circle of candles. A shimmering flash of lightning pierced the surgery from wall to wall but the father did not see it. He was scooping Luke into his arms, turning without a glance at the immortal being so close to him, and running back to the shaking Ginny and Ellie.

Set, his demonic spell apparently broken, blinked his inhuman eyes and staggered a step away from Cort. The thing's tail flicked a last time, knocking several candles to the floor. And the teacher, given a second chance—quickly stooped and seized his fallen talisman. "Give me immortality!" he shrieked, his command ringing with the fanfare clamor of ultimate madness.

Set thundered with rage, his many-clawed paw sweeping through the smoky air, ripping Cort open from throat to genitals in a stroke like that of a master surgeon. The flesh was laid back, in flaps that did not even redden for a moment, did not even permit the organs inside to begin tumbling out for an agonizing second. Then the great claws were stuck in the pelvic bones, and the god raised Cort above his head, shaking, making a rain of *things* which fell from the sundered flesh into Set's welcoming, wide-open jaws.

In the last instant of the human's life he heard the entity scream, "Intense pain opens the way to control of the soul, just as you said—*and now I control yours for eternity!*"

Lightning flashed again in myriad mad bolts that turned the surgery to day—there was a great cloud of stinking, acrid smoke—and both Set and Cort Bellefontaine Devalyn were joined on the pathway to immortality.

EPILOGUE

People who stop at the site of a dreadful automobile accident sometimes take one close look and faint dead away.

Those who have seen injuries up close sometimes suffer the same fate. And more than a few kindly, well-intentioned young fathers-to-be have planned to see their first children into the world of man, only to see the back of their eyelids instead.

But for those few, rare people who are periodically obliged to witness the really *gross* horrors—the fantastic, the grotesque, or the ineffably terrifying—it may well be that the mind prevents immediate acceptance of the sight on the grounds that the witnesses might never resume consciousness. A complete or immediate registering upon the frail spirit of humankind seems to be suspended; or perhaps the witness is allowed to accept what he or she has seen only, slowly, one hyperventillating step at a time.

It was a black and light-swallowing midnight when they went out to the waiting room, the survivors. Alan, Ginny and the freshly widowed Ellie Devalyn did not faint. Instead, feeling unbelievably exhausted—with still-stuporous Luke, Lucy and Brian Devalyn—they sought chairs for their bodies and tears for the relief of their souls.

Time went by, unnoticed. Oddly, they did not fear remaining there. Except for the body of Preston Sumner, the place was empty, and each of the survivors sensed it would stay that way. The only haunts left in the one-story building were those of patients who had been beleaguered with intentional pain, and those fearful ghouls which chittered beneath the conscious level of the survivors' minds.

Each of them sensed that it would be foolishness to try to discuss what had happened. They had no reference points or explanations in their philosophy with which to handle such horror.

Instead, Ginny hugged her friend Ellie and told her how sorry she was that Cort "had to go in such an awful way," then heard the valiant blonde reply with bitter sincerity, "It might be better, this way, in the long run."

Brian Devalyn, in a chair across from the two women, found that the long muscle in his right thigh leapt involuntarily when he heard such remarks. He sighed and it made him shudder. Someday, Brian knew, he would have to sit down and think very carefully about both his father and the grandfather he'd never, thankfully, seen. To consider how well he'd known his Dad, if at all, and much more importantly and frighteningly, to reflect on other matters much closer at hand: Such as, to what degree had an ordinary fourteen-year-old kid named Brian inherited the evil tendencies of the most cruel humans he'd ever known? He didn't think he felt the way Dad, and his father felt; he really didn't; but it was obvious that Dad had gone mad partly because he would not or could not face up to the truth about himself.

For Alan Simmons, there was relief on several levels to confound the horror of his memories. He'd faced the worst and most awesome challenges of his life and, in the process of living up to them, reasserted both his right to be called a father and his own deep reservoir of love for the child who was so different from him. The child who was safe, now.

Then, too, there was the fact that one telephone call to the Indianapolis *News*—after the police came, of course; he'd given them a ring and talked curtly of death only moments ago—would give him a regular position with the big-city newspaper. Hell's bells, if he whispered a smidgen of it to the goddam *New York Times* or *Washington Post* they'd probably take him on, just to get all the facts that were fit (if one didn't read them at the dinner hour) to print.

But he wasn't sure, yet, how he'd play all that. He worked for the tiny suburban *Hossier Subjects*, after all, and he liked to think of himself as a loyal kind of person. They'd probably refuse to handle it, anyway; it didn't have much to do with local merchants and real estate agents and mothers who'd had twins and the latest supermarket specials which were the steady fare of the suburban press. Yeah, they might very well be dumb enough not to publish the story, and then he could contact Willie Dean at the *News*.

. . . Where the hell did Luke run off to?

He was only ten years old but he knew he wouldn't be that size forever, that he was growing right now, taller than he'd been when he was nine. Gosh, was that only a couple of weeks ago? It seemed like forever! He was only ten and he'd seen all those things that most kids never, ever got to see, except at the movies.

But he'd also seen that there really *was* something called Death, that it didn't happen only to bugs you sprayed in the apartment but to people. People he knew.

Except for that, now that the drug ole Uncle Press gave him was wearing off, Luke was feeling just a trifle euphoric. Perhaps he had the right. Why not? He'd had his life threatened, but the threateners were dead instead—at least, one of them was. Where Uncle Cort had gone to was anybody's guess, and Luke didn't want to think about it.

Anyway, *he'd* made it, along with the other kids. And while Cort and Press had been crazy beyond belief, it also seemed true to young Luke that some of the stuff they were after wasn't all that bad. Being likeable, for example, Likeable to Dad. Yeah, some of the stuff the crazies had tried to get made sense in a way.

He forced himself to look down at the body of the dentist, just to satisfy a thread of curiosity about where the ears had gone and then the more challenging problem of stepping over the candle-tallowed circle of death in which Set had appeared.

The Dentist

Luke paused, looking down again. He saw what he wanted and picked it up.

If he understood it properly, what had happened in here, that big Set had come because Cort actually summoned him—which didn't make the teacher any smarter than the other adults Luke knew. Oh sure, Cort thought he was asking someone or something else—Anubis or something. But he'd known that he was dealing with forces that had been around a lot longer than people, and it was just plain stupid to figure he was smarter than they were. Uncle Cort had gotten everything he had coming to him, and so had the dentist. Luke made a face that scorned his ex-captors and went back out to the waiting room.

"There you are."

It was Dad talking, smiling at him. Luke frowned. He'd never seen a smile like that on Dad's face, except maybe when he was talking to Mom. And he was putting out his hands, the way Mom did sometimes, wanting him to go over and put his own hands out to them.

He settled for slipping one small hand into his father's and grinning awkwardly back at Alan.

"I'm so thankful you're safe," Dad said softly, squeezing the hand until it hurt. "I'm going to be more understanding from now on, Luke, I promise you that. What I'm trying to say is, I don't mind, anymore, if you turn out to be smarter than I am. That's the way it should be, for each generation to get smarter than the one before. That's progress, right?"

"Whatever you say, Dad," Luke replied, trying surreptitiously to pull his injured hand free.

"But what really worries me, son, is the horrible things

you've seen tonight." Dad's eyes burned into his with that new affection, that new regard. They beseeched him, pleaded with him to be okay. "Do you think you can learn to handle tonight, Luke? Can you learn to live with it?"

Luke smiled. "Sure, Dad, I think so." With his free hand, he patted the talisman he'd tucked into his pocket. "Somehow I think I'm going to be just fine."

AUTHOR'S NOTE

The Dentist is, in its entirety and clear intention, a work of fiction. None of the characters is based on a living acquaintance of mine, and the character of Doctor Preston Sumner is not based on any member of the dental profession whom I have ever known. It should also be established that I have no particular quarrel to pick with that profession and that its use, in the form of one principal character, was made necessary only by the demands of the storyline.

For the most part, allusions to Egyptian deities and customs are based on researched fact. Certain physical as well as traditional aspects were, however, rearranged or modified for reasons of plot and entertainment.

In closing, by all means see your dentist twice a year for a thorough check-up—but if he has a close friend who's brilliant, teaches anthropology, and carries a talisman, you're on your own!

J. N. Williamson
Indianapolis, Indiana